Acclaim from both sides
of the Atlantic for *The Rationalist*

"Compelling . . . Erotic . . . At every moment the quality of the writing surprises and delights."

—Manchester *Guardian*

"The writing, like Grange himself, is quite beautifully controlled, with teasing lacunae of admirable British discretion. . . . Warwick Collins' novel manages to unite a cold beauty and warm lyrical tone, no mean accomplishment . . . By the time we reach the end, we have experienced an about-face as shocking, yet inevitable, as the one in Neil Jordan's *The Crying Game*."

—*Newsday*

"Titillating and richly evocative . . . [A] hotblooded tale of sweet reason at odds with fleshly delights. . . . A well-crafted, subtle probe of refined men and women called by their sensuality to rebel against convention—at their peril."

—*Kirkus Reviews*

"Vivid and beautifully written."

—*Time Out*

"Here's an erotic, beautifully crafted novel that incorporates two fundamental sexual fantasies . . . I was spellbound from start to finish and delighted to see female lust get the upper hand."

—Val Hennessy
Daily Mail

"There are echoes of *Les Liaisons Dangereuses* and *The French Lieutenant's Woman* here, but Collins manages to avoid all the clichés. This is a novel full of passion and ideas . . . Collins is totally in command of his material. The tension is sustained as much by his beautifully realised sense of place as the emotional high wire act we're forced to witness."

—*Midweek*

"A compelling study of passion . . . An intimate depiction of sexual obsession all the more seductive for its air of rational detachment . . . *The Rationalist* may well prove to be one of the most promising novels of the year."

—*Spectator*

"Highly diverting."

—*Independent on Sunday*

ALSO BY WARWICK COLLINS

CHALLENGE
NEW WORLD
DEATH OF AN ANGEL

The Rationalist

A NOVEL

WARWICK COLLINS

Ballantine Books • New York

Library of Congress Catalog Card Number: 94-94566

ISBN: 0-345-39185-3

Cover design by Barbara Leff
Cover painting of Lady Hamilton as Circe (c.1782) by George Romney. Copyright © Tate Gallery, London/Art Resource, NY

Manufactured in the United States of America

First Ballantine Books Edition: February 1995

10 9 8 7 6 5 4 3 2 1

The
Rationalist

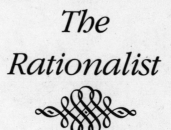

All knowledge is tentative.
—Karl Popper

1

As the ritual began, Dr. Silas Grange observed his hands washing one another with soap and water. He might be above himself, floating. His hands might be fishes. Detached, he regarded them curling around one another. As if from a distance, he was aware of the gurgle and hiss as he poured a jug of clear rainwater over first one and then the other to remove the soap. He heard the reverberant clang of the metal jug as it was replaced. In silent concentration he observed both hands, rising from the water, dry themselves upon a towel.

In the style of the day, Grange wore no wig. His hair was drawn back straight and ended in a small pigtail. His shirt, cleanly pressed by Mrs. Thompson, glowed obscure white beneath his direct vision. While his hands dried themselves, he glanced upward. In the small mirror on the ledge above the metal handbasin, his face appeared to him cold, reserved, thoughtful.

At nine Grange began work, calling in his first patient, Obadiah Pitt. He approached the elderly foundryman with a burning candle held close by, looking into his eye. Pitt was overseer on the evening shift at the iron foundry at Sowley, perhaps three miles away. As Grange approached more closely with the candle, he observed how the flame flickered in the liquid surface of the foundryman's eye. In Grange's gaze, Obadiah Pitt's eye seemed to detach itself from his body. (Thus the mind abstracts the object of its focus.) Grange's hand approached the eye with a pair of tweezers and, pausing at the reflection of the flame, removed a minuscule object like a tiny iron worm.

"A metal splinter," Grange commented. "Can you see?"

He placed the tweezers on a metal tray. The foundryman blinked. Grange, standing in front of his seated patient, clapped his hands once, authoritatively. Pitt glanced toward him suddenly, as if from a daydream.

"Can you see?" Grange repeated.

Obadiah Pitt blinked several times, nodded, gave a half smile. Grange smiled back. It was a tight smile, circumscribed, a professional smile, imparting confidence but little warmth.

When Pitt had left, he began again by washing, observing the movement of the hands as they struggled against one another to make themselves clean. He reached for the jug and heard, as it might be from the other side of the room, the water being poured.

Again he experienced the faintly uncomfortable sensation of perceiving himself as if from a distance. Focusing upon his thoughts, he became detached, an entity of the mind. Merely to anchor himself, he glanced again at the mirror, though he was not much interested in what he saw there. He noticed, as if observing another person, that his expression as he dried his hands was neutral, perhaps a little sardonic, secure in his profession.

"Here?" Grange asked.

He moved his hand along the boundary of Miss Chine's swollen belly. "Here?" His hand moved again, drifting on the circumference of the world. "You must help me, if you can, Miss Chine."

Mary Chine, pregnant, lay back in magnificence on a chair while Grange ran his palm carefully across her stomach. Her face indicated more fear than embarrassment.

"Here?"

Miss Chine turned her head away and coughed, a sound like a mew. Grange asked again, "Here, then?"

He removed his hand.

"I do not think it is what you fear. No hobgoblin or strange spirit affects your pregnancy, but an infection of the bile. You are overworking, I fancy. I will write a note to your employer, requesting five days' leave."

Miss Chine pulled down her voluminous skirts and raised herself upright. Grange walked to his desk, sat down, dipped quill in ink and wrote briskly on a single sheet. He signed it, then took it between thumb and forefinger and waved it to dry the ink. If his client had been richer, and he had wanted to impress, he would have poured a little fine sand to dry it. But Miss Chine was sent to him under the auspices of the poorhouse, aided now by Mrs. Quill and her committee. The note having dried, he folded it on the desk and handed it to her, rising from his desk to nod goodbye. With hardly an acknowledgment, she tucked it into the sleeve of her dress. Even now, she seemed unable to speak. Her nervousness in his presence appeared profound. He suspected it was his elaborate courtesy which caused this fear, courtesy being a barrier to the emotions, a means of hiding his great and benevolent coldness.

As she left, he nodded to another figure sitting in the small alcove that served as a waiting area. A man in his mid-thirties entered, strongly built, perhaps slightly nervous, not facing Grange but sideways on.

"Mister . . . ?"

"Swann, sir."

"Mr. Swann . . . You are a seaman, I think?"

"Second mate, sir, merchantman."

"What ails you?"

"My arm, sir."

"If you would take off your shirt."

As Swann presently stood, he was sideways on to the physician. He removed his shirt with his closest arm. Then, out of an obscure belligerence born perhaps of shyness, he swung to face Grange. It was a dramatic, even a theatrical gesture, heightened by the evidence of what he had to show. His left arm was a stump, severed at the elbow. At its tip was a black substance—pitch.

Grange from his calm height regarded him carefully, choosing his words. "I perceive you have a problem with your arm, Mr. Swann."

"Letting out anchor, sir, a fortnight ago in weather, on the *Limpet*, two hundred tons." Grange swung his gaze from the arm to Swann's face. "Caught my arm in a bight. Wire, not rope—rope's kinder. Dipped it in pitch to stop the blood. It begins to hurt a little, now."

"Hurts a little," Grange repeated. "Raise your arm."

Veins and arteries off color, he noted to himself; a pale color to the skin in the proximal area.

"Lower now," Grange admonished.

He pinched Swann's arm at the shoulder. "Does this hurt?"

"No, sir."

"This?"

Lower down, the flesh appeared stolid and unyielding.
"This?"

Swann's face emptied with pain. Grange glanced at him.
"Good. It's not well advanced."

"Not well advanced, sir?"

"Gangrene."

Swann bit his lip. A change came over Grange. In the
absence of anesthetics, a doctor or surgeon must rely instead
on force of character. He must create a drama in which the
patient is a willing participant. Grange, usually taciturn, became more brisk.

"I merely confirm what you know, Mr. Swann. You're a
brave man, I think. You've saved your life by not delaying.
We shall need to amputate the arm close to the shoulder. I
have your cooperation?"

Swann nodded, though not with enthusiasm.

"You can have my arm, sir. Not much use to me, swaying
in the breeze."

"I'll accept your offer, then."

Grange nodded. As if only now seized by the momentum of
what he would undertake, he turned and walked to the door,
calling out loudly downstairs:

"Mrs. Thompson!"

A few seconds later, Mrs. Thompson's rubicund face
floated into view at the bottom of the stairs.

"Sir?"

"Amputation. Prepare hot pitch, if you please."

"Hot pitch, sir?"

"Directly."

Grange reentered the surgery. In order to distract Swann,
to maintain the pace, he must act with panache. He walked to
a side cabinet and opened a drawer. Taking hold of a strong
piece of cord, he closed the drawer with an emphatic sweep.

"I am going to apply a tourniquet. As a seaman, I ask you
what knot I should use for best effect. I used to work on boats
in my youth, to pay my way. Captain Lerman, the *Feather*.
Ferry packet . . ."

Swann nodded, with a nervous smile.

"Nothing wrong with the *Feather*. A constrictor knot, sir. Do you know it?"

"Let me see now. You test me, Mr. Swann. I do believe . . . Is it a clove hitch with . . . an extra tuck under the adjacent?"

"Under the opposite, sir. But for that, you have it properly. You can tighten and tighten and it won't spring out."

Grange approached him with the cord.

"Hold out your arm."

He formed a clove hitch on Swann's shoulder, then looped the cord under the opposite, forming a constrictor knot, and tightened.

"Harder, sir. That way you'll numb my arm so I won't feel a thing."

Grange gave a brief smile of approval. Wrapping the two strands of the cord around the palm of each hand, he closed his fists. With a grunt he used his full strength to wrench the cord brutally tight. Swann let out a keening sound in his throat that ended in a cough.

"Shout as much as you like, Mr. Swann." Grange was speaking to himself now, engrossed in his actions. "No one will hear you except Mrs. Thompson."

Exultant, sweating, Swann said: "I'll sing for her then, sir."

For safety's sake, Grange tied another cord around Swann's arm just beneath the shoulder. With a savage jerk he tightened it. Swann almost fainted with pain. Grange was working fast now, making additional loops, giving a series of further sudden jerks which seemed to punctuate his sentences.

"You're a seaman, and I'll tell you straight. I could hack you at the shoulder, at the bone's join. But you wouldn't fit so well into your jacket for the ladies. So I'm going to cut down the arm an inch or two for your tailor's sake."

"The ladies, sir. My tailor, sir. Thank you, sir."

"In the interests of preserving a pretty figure, you understand. Cutting through the bone will take a little longer. So sing well."

"I'll do my best, sir."

Approaching the largest cupboard, Grange opened a door, removed a bottle and an iron mug, and poured a heavy dose of rum into the mug. He handed it to Swann. Swann nodded and drank in great gulps. He handed the mug back to Grange. Grange refilled it. Swann drank again, spilling some down the side of his mouth. He wiped his lips with his free hand, blinked.

Grange was all energy now, one movement driving without respite into the next. He strode rather than walked to a sideboard, kneeled, pulled out from beneath it a wooden toolbox case, and withdrew from the box a short saw and a heavy, strong-bladed knife. Inside were scrapes, blades, lances, and screws, a crude toolbox for the human anatomy. Grange turned away and with quick sweeps sharpened the knife on a whetstone. It was another emphatic gesture designed to fill the silence while Mrs. Thompson heated the pitch. The patient waits, the whetstone sings. Behind the sound of the blade, Mrs. Thompson's footsteps approached up the stairs. She entered with the boiling pitch in a steaming open basin.

Grange placed the sharpened knife on the table, threw an adjacent wall curtain briskly back, and hauled out what seemed a battered wooden carpenter's trestle, covered in dark stains. He dragged it toward the center of the room.

"Prepare for battle, Mr. Swann. We need your arm across this trestle."

Swann nodded. The fear had risen like whiteness into his gills, but there was a force and progression in what they were about to do. Under his own momentum, he moved without apparent hesitation to the trestle, kneeled, placed his arm across it. Grange pulled a chair away from the table, turning it so that Swann could lean on it. Swann put the elbow of his right arm on the chair, and gripped its back with his one hand to prevent himself fainting. Now, as Grange crossed behind him to take position beside the trestle, it seemed to him as if Swann were praying.

So it was that Grange took firm hold of the saw, glanced at Mrs. Thompson standing by with the pitch, and observed that she too was white but composed.

He nodded toward his assistant, a brief recognition. Mrs. Thompson swallowed and nodded back. Grange's face tightened as he braced himself.

"Battle stations, Mr. Swann."

The sawing was plain and terrible. A sound emerged from Swann as the trestle itself seemed to roar and groan and then screamed. It continued for perhaps ten seconds, and for Grange it seemed as always like eternity until the calm, implacable thud of the stump hitting the large metal receptacle signaled its physical termination. Grange lowered the bloody saw, lifted the knife from the table, and swiftly cut hanging flesh. Blood spurted onto his trousers. He made several rapid stitches into the skin with needle and thread. The focus of his mind was on the task, all other matters held at bay. His head jerked once or twice as he worked swiftly.

Swann was making a howling, singing sound. Grange grasped the pitch bowl in one hand and with the other handed the receptacle with the stump to Mrs. Thompson. Whitefaced, she covered the receptacle with a cloth and placed it on the sideboard. Then she leaned forward to prevent the kneeling Swann from falling over.

Swann was making deep sobs and sighs, almost like a man asleep. Now some obscure force in him was rising. He was starting to sing for Mrs. Thompson. Grange kneeled and applied boiling pitch with a pestle to the bloody stump. Swann screamed and choked, then began to sing again. Beneath his direct vision, Grange's shirt became casually red with spurts of blood as he applied the pitch. Eventually Grange halted and breathed in deeply. The stump was sealed and blackened.

Grange rose, ignoring the sudden cramp in his knee, and walked round to Swann's other side. He placed Swann's remaining arm around his shoulder and heaved him to his feet.

He and Mrs. Thompson half lifted, half dragged Swann to the low surgical bed at the corner of the room. They lowered him carefully, but even as they did so Swann cried out once more, a terrible sound, like a man who has lost his child; after which he was silent.

2

"No bandages, Mrs. Thompson," Grange ordered. "The pitch needs cool air to harden."

He leaned down toward the patient.

"Can you hear me, Mr. Swann? Battle's over."

Swann's faced appeared pallid, covered in sweat. He moved his lips:

"Over . . ."

Mrs. Thompson spread a blanket over his recumbent body. Swann's shoulder overhung the floor. Kneeling, Mrs. Thompson placed a bowl on the bare boards beneath the stump to collect blood. Swann seemed settled.

Grange nodded toward Mrs. Thompson, who sailed calmly white to the sideboard, lifted the covered iron receptacle with the stump, and turned to the door. Grange followed her, casually rubbing his bloodstained hands with a rag. On the landing, he closed the door behind him.

Mrs. Thompson was facing away and about to descend the stairs, but when she heard Grange's voice, she halted. Rubbing his hands with the rag, in a low voice Grange informed her:

"I must visit several patients this afternoon, and I have an engagement to see Dr. Hargood this evening. Will you bury Mr. Swann's arm . . . deep?"

"Of course, sir."

Out of obduracy, Grange lowered his voice still further.

"There is a tale of a man from Brightlingsea, Mrs. Thompson, who had the same operation. Several days later, he was walking up a narrow lane when he met a mongrel coming from the opposite direction. The dog carried in its mouth a familiar article . . . A brisk tug-of-war ensued over a matter of lost property."

"You're cheerful today, sir," Mrs. Thompson observed.

"Let Mr. Swann sleep there as long as he likes. He's a strong man, and will demand to go in a few hours or so. Tell him to keep indoors for several days, to wrap well, no chills or drafts."

"Sir."

"When he wakes, allow him as much rum as he likes. Rum makes some men surly. A sailor is the opposite. He becomes surly without."

"Yes, sir."

Released, Mrs. Thompson went downstairs. Grange opened the door again, observed that the patient was settled, though now Swann was shaking visibly beneath his blankets. Grange walked past him to a high cupboard, removed a bottle of rum and filled the iron mug. He pulled up a small table toward Swann, placed the bottle and the filled mug there. Apart from his constant shivering, Swann showed no further signs of movement. Grange listened for a little while longer to Swann's breathing, then went to his study.

In the confines of his study, a shudder passed through Grange, the exaltation of his terror having passed. A perturbation grew in his body's core, at his heart or spine, and moved outward. It seemed to shake his body like quake or tremor, moving from his rib cage and sternum outward into his limbs, so that he observed its final tremble in his forearms, wrists, and hands. As a snake might leave its skin, so in this single, instinctive shudder his body seemed to slough off its hidden terror and transmitted shock. In his earlier days he had been sick with a kind of relief, and afterward felt exactly this formal lightness. Now he drew in air heavily, and closed his eyes for several seconds.

He prepared to wash again. His bloodstained shirt and trousers lay soaking in a bowl of water that Mrs. Thompson had brought up for the task before she dealt with the matter of the stump. He paused, looking down his arms to his hands, which he now examined with detached interest. Beneath the gaze his hands were still shaking. There was a part of him that remained separate, even when he was looking at himself, at his own infirmities. He knew this shaking was to be expected, and half smiled in melancholy recognition. Before the final trembling had gone, he began to wash his hands carefully and methodically.

Though he had been taught at Edinburgh the requirements of cleanliness, yet he suspected that much of its appeal to him resided in the ritual, the formal piety of washing. After the mayhem of surgery, the only sounds were the sluice of fresh water and the clatter of the water jug as it was replaced.

Having observed the niceties of cleaning his hands, he splashed water on his face and washed his forehead, jaw, and neck, before rubbing his face and neck briskly with a clean towel. Pausing to blink and glance at himself in the mirror, he saw reflected in its surface the window that opened onto Lymington High Street. From the far side of the street it appeared that two women were talking decorously, leaning toward one another under parasols, so that their attitudes impeccably counterbalanced one another. Under his brief and curious gaze they clarified themselves into Mrs. Angela Hudson and Mrs. Celia Quill. He must have caught sight of them at the end of their conversation, for they nodded to one another and parted, Mrs. Hudson walking toward the upper street and St. Thomas, Mrs. Quill in the other direction, toward the river bridge and Walhampton.

He was left with an impression of the grace of Mrs. Quill's carriage as she turned away, her gliding walk, the confident and discreet angle of her parasol, before she passed out of the window's ambit. He experienced a passing urge to watch her departure further, but restrained himself from walking to the window in order to gain the requisite view. Besides, he was bare to the waist, and it seemed unseemly to risk showing himself, despite the fringe of discreet lace that Mrs. Thompson had placed across the window precisely so that he could change without due concern about being overlooked from the street.

With the image of Mrs. Quill turning still in his mind, he drew on a new shirt from the cupboard constantly replenished by Mrs. Thompson, and with his fingers began to do up the buttons, starting at the top and working downward. He sat on the chair to pull on his trousers, stood up to haul them to his waist and adjust the breech. He tied a scarf around his neck, then put on his jacket, brushing his hair.

A short while afterward he stepped out of his study, opened the door to the room in which Swann was uneasily sleeping or perhaps fainted, and listened to his breathing for several seconds. Closing the door, he walked down the stairs in his stockinged feet, preparatory to putting on the leather boots that he used to walk his rounds and that were kept by the door for the purpose.

In the hallway, Grange halted and stood for a moment. He

could hear, in the background, Mrs. Thompson bustling about.

Mrs. Thompson called cheerfully, "You are departing, sir?"

He sat in the tall chair in the hallway to pull on his boots. "If there is any adverse circumstance with Mr. Swann, you know that I shall be returning before five."

"I shall keep an eye on him, sir."

Grange opened the front door and stepped through. Outside, the sun was fierce. He had a brief image of the efficacy of Mrs. Quill's parasol. The sunlight drove under his narrowed lids like light beneath a door. He paused and raised his hand against its brightness. Sunlight rode over his hand and through his fingers. After several seconds of adjustment, he lowered his hand. Then he began to walk down Lymington Hill and turned right along a footpath toward Edred Wright's small house at Woodford, perhaps four hundred yards distant.

3

*H*e had insisted, in the early days of his career, that he ply his trade in Lambeth.

It was a district of suffering air, lit, like the streets themselves, by incongruous visitations. The winged heads on the tombstones did not represent ascended angels, but souls hovering in that abyss between death and resurrection. London seemed to him the long interval between lives. If Grange pictured Hell at all, it was perhaps like this, people drifting like leaves, houses crouched back to back, an army of souls that were pressed so thickly together they were upon the earth like an overlay of grime.

Yet life was inextricable from change, bodily growth, and decay. Some aspect of the city seemed full of furtive movement. The streets were filled with shadows, the air itself crumbled and held him. Once, walking along the Mortlake, through one of those interminable back streets on a hazy afternoon, he had heard a shriek of despair, a single rising scream, as if a soul were striving to escape. He had continued to walk into the afternoon, but something inside him felt unhinged. As he traveled he felt his terror grow. He knew he would leave London, then, to practice in the country.

It was perhaps deeper than a mere emotional revulsion. The very image of London, London the collector of peoples, London the center of all trade, offended his notions of the pursuit of the truth to which, inadvertently or not, he felt committed. London was too close to humanity itself, to its beating heart; one would be smothered by its demands, not on the body (he was lucky in having a reasonably sound constitution) but on the mind, or to put it more directly, on the character. What he sought was distance, a reasonable living in which he might do some small good for his fellow man, and could make time for his other studies.

His own strict image of the truth, learned in the academies of Scotland, was central to this notion. One could not use the image of a candle shedding its light upon objects, for the truth seemed to emerge from the inside like some internal radiance, as ghostly as the patina on silver. It appeared to him that truth was not prolix or voluble, but crept out shyly from the side, like a man escaping from a house. The crowd might gather at the front door, waiting for its bold announcement and popular delivery, but they were unlikely to observe its calm egress. Objectivity, for him, was the ability to stand aside from the crowd, and survey the facts coldly and surreptitiously for oneself. This was the scientist's view, at least as he understood it, and to practice it required distance. It was at the same time the root of his detachment and the root too (though he might not admit it directly) of his bachelordom.

Yet in the pursuit of this vague notion, he knew that he had committed his soul to a mystery as perplexing as any inchoate divinity. Truth was seldom, if ever, actual; it escaped the direct grasp. It resembled instead the flickering of a dream. He knew only this for certain: All truth was an approximation. In this he found both comfort and despair.

"Speak then," Grange suggested.

Edred Wright breathed softly, gathering himself. As he shifted, Grange detected a whiff of his body, a stale smell of sweat and urine mixed with the odor of a sore. His body had accumulated scars, mostly concentrated on the hands and wrists, but also on the elbows and knees from hauling himself through the bilges of great ships. In the sawpits sometimes a terrible wound was inflicted casually and quickly, with the saw's shark teeth. The pay of shipwrights was double that of laborers, for good reason. Most of the men who worked at Buckler's Hard were contract men. As each new ship began, the demand for labor rose and fell like the tides. There was also the nearby ironworks at Sowley, which made pig iron. Men laid off from Buckler's Hard sometimes found temporary employment there.

Edred Wright's voice was hardly discernible as he whispered, "I have difficulty breathing. My body's rotting." He looked around him in the gloom, his flesh like the yellow light of tallow. On a crude oak table were two lamps, with pepperpot holes in the back for oxygen, a wicker birdcage with a wren, several earthenware pots, an open sack of potatoes.

"Am I dying?"

"We are all dying," Grange said. "You have a daughter?"

"Yes."

He needs someone, Grange thought, to replace dressings on the sores. Close by, the smell was strong.

"I will call by daily, now."

"I am dying, then." There was a note of relief, almost, in

Wright's voice. The sores were troublesome, but the spirit was no longer willing. It was strange how easily people departed. Grange had seen perhaps thirty people die in the last year, mainly from the smallpox. He recalled them briefly, a series of masks or painted faces, through a foreground of quiet activity which did not much help, but perhaps ameliorated the incongruity of watching another person leave this world.

"Where is your daughter?"

"She's gone, sir."

"She neglects you."

"I neglected her."

He felt a sudden twinge of sympathy for Wright, his lack of self-pity. It was something he had observed in most trades to do with the sea, even in shipwrights, at second remove.

"You could live," Grange suggested, "if you wished."

"If I wished," Wright whispered. His eyes, turned upward, reminded Grange of pike he had seen in his youth, utterly without expression, or rather, the expression of an old predator who is somehow indifferent to his fate.

Outside the back door was a dovecote, broken, and several empty hives. Everything living had died or departed, except, perhaps, the lice.

By contrast, at Mrs. Eldon's bedside he felt something like irritation. After his examination of Mrs. Eldon, her daughter Augusta hovered anxiously on the other side of the bed, a disembodied spirit. Grange sensed her desire to speak, but did not have it in his heart to allow her, to set her at rest. She accompanied Grange to the hallway, closing the bedroom door behind her, staring anxiously into his face when he turned to face her.

"Well?"

Grange's eyes drifted around the room. There were objects there from all around the Empire, the result of the wanderings of Mrs. Eldon's husband, a former diplomat. The prime impression was that the interior was full of priceless works of art, the second that not a speck of dust had been allowed even to float near them. But at the third look the place had a more dowdy feel, and it lay perhaps in the fact that the collection appeared to be governed by no single thought or strategy. Eldon had clearly been a man who had a collector's urge but not much scientific or literary learning. There was a jackdaw quality to his selection, porcelain and minerals, objects of *virtu* and icons, masks and small pagan deities. A wall carried stuffed trophies, deerheads and the hand of an apelike being. The bookshelves held a few abbreviated runs of leather and gilt volumes.

"I believe your mother is improving, Miss Eldon."

"She's not eating, doctor."

"You mean, I think, that she's not eating five meals a day."

"She eats only two . . ."

"At her age one would be enough," Grange informed.

"But . . ."

"And what about you? Are you eating enough? You seem to pine."

A blush floated across Mistress Eldon's fine if somewhat anemic features. Grange was always surprised at the immediacy of female blushes; a contradiction in terms, a creeping suddenness, there briefly like a cloud's shadow. He wondered about its physiology. It was as if an emotion had struck something and returned, flinging red into neck, face, and hands.

"I am well enough, sir."

"You are sure?"

A devil inside him hoped to see another blush across her pale white skin, traces of the sun between. She bit her lower lip, resisting. He should not flirt with her, yet something in him was satisfied and released.

Now she had recovered and stared at him clearly, as if daring him to mock her further. Nodding and bowing briefly, he turned away. As he descended the spiral staircase he heard her soft footsteps behind him, a fluttering shadow over his own.

At the threshold he turned and nodded again, then the door liberated him to the exterior.

. . .

The day, mercifully, had lost some of its heat. Long afternoon shadows lay on the fields. There was a calm time in the late afternoon when the trees and hedgerows seemed hushed, as if the birds and insects were recovering from the exhaustion of a summer's day. The faintest of sea breezes stirred the leaves. Grange loosened his neckerchief and began to walk back to Lymington.

Several goats were tethered beside a lonely group of cottages at Oxey Barn. Although smoke issued from one of the chimneys, no human could be seen. Driftwood was piled untidily on a corner of one of the plots. Not far from the Chequers public house three men crossed his path, walking purposefully toward the shoreline. They were silent, spread out perhaps ten feet abreast, and they made no acknowledgment of him as they passed. He glanced back surreptitiously to study their progress. They were moving downhill, and already their heavy boots splashed in the saturated marsh ground. Seabirds rose in alarm as they crossed an open water meadow, walking toward the Pennington shoreline.

The people here appeared morose to outsiders. It was one of those closed communities which, though peaceful, were outside the law. A long, slow feud between two families, Rickmans and Wrights, was like a peat fire which continues underground but cannot be put out. He saw some of its effects; stab wounds in the side of a Rickman boy, which the victim would not discuss; a young woman—cousin to the Wrights—distraught from the loss of her child, yet unable to voice her suspicions over its asphyxiation. The district produced occasional casualties amongst the adult males. Several years previously the body of Ebenezer Briggs, a bagman, was found beneath a sea wall, his throat neatly slit and his limbs oddly twisted. Yet the law did not have to investigate further into the intricacies of the feud. The culprit was delivered sullenly into its hands, as if by common consent, and the community again closed its ranks.

He continued through the district of Woodside. The seaward side was an area of open marsh, broken only—along the shore—by the pitched roof of an occasional salt boilerhouse. There he paused briefly to stare out over the flashes of open water, estuaries, and mudbanks. Water calmed him. He needed only to survey its surface and the changing light above it to experience its benign influence on his soul. There he could forget, for a short while, the agitations which sometimes rose up inside him, not least his suspicion that his patient Edred Wright had been deserted by his clan for some obscure reason and simply left like an old, grounded whale to die. It was part of that ancient, irrational element of which, as a modern man, he quietly despaired.

After a few minutes of solemn contemplation of the water, the shifting seabirds, he returned to the house in the early evening to change, somewhat the better for his brief sojourn at the water's edge.

4

*A*cross the dark foreground of the meadows, the Solent was a glimmering white, like the wake of a ship. Behind it rose the high shoreline of the Isle of Wight. Walking briskly along the footpath, beside Walhampton Fields, Grange could see against the mass of the island foreshore two tiny points of light, the great braziers on the piers at Yarmouth.

The Solent and its geography did not, for the moment,

concern him. His gaze was cast lower, as he tried to penetrate the depths of the incoming night. Taking care not to stumble into a ditch or stagnant pool, he searched bushes and the low hedgerows, looking for that telltale greenish white light which signified *Lampyris noctiluca*, the glowworm, though it was in fact the female, wingless form of the beetle that used light to signal to flying males. He had an obsession with the mysteries of light. Once, in a hedgerow near Oxey, he found a bush which winked in the gloaming with females of *Lampyris*, perhaps a dozen. He had approached it dry-mouthed, watching its ghostly pulsations with that concentration of attention in which all else is excluded, except this tiny universe of lovers signaling for their mates.

Tonight he could see no sign of *Lampyris*, though his eyes began to water with the strain of peering into the dark ditches and deeper shadows. Finding no reward for his endeavors, he raised his attention once more to the band of coastline where the water held the last vestiges of luminescence. It was at this time of year that gales and storms sometimes thrashed the coast. When wind was against tide, huge waves built up on the Brambles and toward the Needles. But now, above the darkness of the ground, the water was a calm unearthly white.

Expecting Grange at nine, Dr. Hargood had hung a tallow lantern outside the door. In the half-light, Hargood's Palladian house, with its pillars, was a ghostly pile. To his right, Grange noticed the outlines of several grazing horses, and heard their shifting hooves as they drifted through the meadow. Already dew had collected on the grass. He could feel its wetness through his leather boots as the lantern flickered and drew him forward to the porch. Although it was not yet dark, several large moths hovered in the outer circles of illumination.

Approaching the porticoed entrance, he raised the bronze knocker and listened to a door being closed inside, then heavy footsteps across the stone flags of the hall until the main door opened, suddenly and peremptorily. Hargood, Grange's colleague and collaborator, squinted at him amiably in the half-light.

"Wraith, come in."

In the hallway Hargood placed a hand on Grange's shoulder and escorted him across the flagstones.

"You had a good trip to London, I trust?" Grange asked.

"I had. Five days there, five days back, and a week of bliss in between."

They walked through to the dining room.

"Your mistress is well?" Grange asked.

"In fine fettle."

In the dining room, two places had been set. Hargood threw out an arm to indicate a chair on the right-hand side of the long table. Hargood sat at the head. "We shall begin directly. I am hungry enough. Simmons!" Hargood called out. "Our guest is here."

"Sir!" Simmons shouted back from the kitchen, a pale echo of Hargood's stentorian roar. Simmons and his wife were Hargood's only servants in the large house. They were a discreet pair, or perhaps it was that they simply preferred to live on the outer fringes of Hargood's booming voice. In his many visits to Hargood's house, Grange had only caught sight of Mrs. Simmons, a small, rotund woman, on a few occasions, but the order of the house spoke well of her attentions.

"Wine, sir?"

"Thank you."

Hargood poured two glasses from a decanter, and for several moments seemed absorbed in observing the color of the liquid as they filled the glasses.

"You are as thin as always," Hargood said, without looking up.

Grange had learned, through long acquaintance, that it was advisable never to object to Hargood's observations about his person. Any sign of resistance would simply cause his senior colleague to press those observations further. Rather, it was advisable to accept them and move on.

"And you, Hargood? You appear in rude good health."

Hargood put down the decanter and leaned forward on the table, lowering his voice conspiratorially: "I am struck dumb by the appearances in London. There are already, amongst the younger women, fashions which I understand have come over from France, from Madame Récamier and Madame Tallien. *Les Merveilleuses*, I believe their followers are called. Slim, high-waisted muslin or cotton gowns, which cling to the figure, which are so simple that they resemble the dresses of young girls—from whose influence I believe they largely derive. They wear flesh-colored tights beneath them, the material of the dresses being so thin you can see through them as through a window."

"Hargood, you paint a charming picture."

"Perhaps. But I begin to feel my age. Gone are the elaborate hair, high heels, jewelry, cosmetics, and corsets which I knew in my youth. In the interests of fashion, all have been ruthlessly discarded in favor of this simplicity of form. In my day, women would rustle with a thousand brocades. Damn it, you hunted a woman through her clothes, sir, you pursued her through a field of whispering silk, like a vixen to her warren. And since she knew the terrain, she had some advantage, I can tell you. That was the game. Now it is all gone."

"Yet," Grange said, "the modern woman is more difficult to fathom?"

Hargood slid one of the two filled glasses toward Grange. The gesture, though swift, did not interrupt the flow of his discourse.

"Women's ears are attuned to fashion as a dog is to a high whistle. They hear its advance and adjust before even you are aware. My own young lady is hardly different. She drags me out to view these *précieuses* parading in the park."

"Does she?"

"Indeed," Hargood affirmed, raising his glass to his nose and sniffing the surface of the wine.

"Yet," Grange riposted, "I hear that only the most advanced

are thus attired. It seems to me that your horse has been spooked, sir, and you have been thrown."

"How so, you young blackguard?"

"The vixen shows herself almost naked, and you are ready to faint away."

"You mock an old rake, sir, at your peril," Hargood said, delighted. "One day your own teeth will be drawn."

But it was a characteristic of Hargood that his mind did not long remain on any one thing. When Simmons, moving more sideways than forward, had carried in the leg of beef, setting it down in front of Hargood ready to be carved, and had retreated silently through the door, Hargood commented as he began to ply the knife: "Silas, my dear fellow, you are too masculine. You have no indulgences, no pleasant vices, at least that I can perceive. You have a mind as cold as winter."

"It is you, rather, who are a romantic," Grange answered. "For myself . . ."

"Yes?" Hargood's knife moved among the meat, his eye following the movement of the blade with absorption.

". . . I consider myself to be a man who is not so much at liberty with his own emotions."

"Fearful, I believe . . ."

"Fearful, perhaps. But this very fear is not entirely to my disadvantage. It preserves a little freedom to pursue other matters which are of interest to me."

"Your damn dry books. You are honest, I do not doubt. Yet I repeat to you, in this fearfulness there is detachment."

"But detachment, if it were possible, is an ideal, is it not? Think of it, Hargood, to conduct one's life by means of logic, rather than the emotions. If that were only possible. To be driven by the intellect, rather than the senses."

"But without the senses, there is no intellect. That is the mistake of those revolutionaries on the other side of the Channel. The intellect alone is a loose gun. It ends up by destroying those who would deploy it."

As if conforming with his words, slices of rich, bloody beef fell away from Hargood's knife. Grange, too close to the early events of the day, glanced away from the slicing, probing blade. Even so, his evening walk to Hargood's house had given him appetite, and the beef was strong in his nostrils.

"Emotions live with us, Silas." Hargood handed Grange a piled plate. "They are our constant companions, whether we like them or not. They inhabit us as much as we inhabit them. Once we recognize them, we have a chance at least of becoming happy."

"Emotions?" Grange asked. "We have a poor, mad King who was pursued through his rooms by Dr. Willis and his band of restraining thugs because he suffered an excess of emotions."

"A merely temporary lapse. When he emerges from these bouts, he is a good sovereign."

"True," Grange admitted. He did not like to agree with Hargood too much, for he was inclined in a Whiggish direction. Accordingly, he would prefer not to admit that the sovereign was popular.

Hargood began to fill his own plate with meat.

"You are in good health, I think. Yet you seem preoccupied."

"Today, unfortunately, I had little recourse but to amputate a man's arm."

"You need some further wine, then. Perhaps you are shaken."

"No, not shaken. It is matter of the soul, rather."

"The soul?"

"An arm is such a large part of the body, like the bough of a tree. The man sang bravely while I undertook the operation. I thought of his soul sundering as his arm hit the dish. It made a terrible, calm sound."

Hargood paused in his carving.

"Damn me, Silas, you must not be morbid. A doctor should feel no guilt. It is important for his well-being. We take risks, for the sake of the patient's health, and some of those attempts will fail. So be it. Afterward we should sleep well."

. . .

Grange cut and chewed his meat carefully. Hargood harried, tore, and consumed, grunting with satisfaction as he progressed.

"You worry, sometimes, about the failures?" Grange asked between mouthfuls.

"One should not be too much concerned. For myself, I have occasionally thought of mine own accounts. According to such, for which God is my witness, in person I have saved perhaps two or three lives a year over the last thirty years. Let us say sixty souls. Set against this, I believe that actions committed on my part, to my best ability, but perhaps without fully understanding the true causes or conditions, may have hastened perhaps five souls to their deaths. Let us be generous, however. Let us say I have caused, as part of my best efforts, and without knowing, double that number of deaths—shall we say a round dozen?"

"You speak most freely."

"Indeed, that is my point. We must be robust. A round dozen to their deaths, then. I think of the scales, and were it not for my intervention, a minimum of sixty would have died, and perhaps because of my presence, a maximum of twelve have departed. I believe, if you will forgive me, that is a reasonable score and balance."

"I admire the honesty of your assessment. But can one score human lives?"

"Yes." Hargood gulped his wine. "Yes indeed. And for precisely this reason. One life is worth exactly another. No more, no less. That is what our profession teaches. It is our ideal. But its consequences, I say, are exact. That is to say, *if*, I repeat, *if* there are sixty saved, twelve dispatched, then I am exactly forty-eight to the good."

"You will go to Heaven, I am sure," Grange observed, adding slyly, "though it may be on a second-class seat."

"As long as it is not to Hell on a first-class seat, I will have no complaints." In good humor, Hargood filled his mouth with meat and chewed amiably. "But why, if the prospect of your patient's condition seems to concern you, did you not send him to a surgeon?"

"I could have sent him to John Colley, I suppose. But Colley is of the old school, one of the barber-surgeons. Of his last dozen amputations, four have subsequently died. If I sent the patient to Salisbury, on the other hand, he would have had to wait for some days, perhaps several weeks, for Henry Leman. Or to Winchester, perhaps longer for James Durrant. Gangrene, once it begins, drives swiftly."

"Colley's patients died of infection?"

"I believe he does not wash all remaining cadaverous traces off his hands. In that distinction, of course, he is no worse and no better than many of the old barber-surgeons. He merely does as ancient practice suggests. At Edinburgh, we were taught that the sources of infection can be smaller than the human eye can perceive . . ."

"Yes, yes." Grange's fellowship of the Royal College of Physicians of Edinburgh rendered Hargood no less suspicious of Scottish universities. "But perhaps I should ask you, what if your patient dies on you?"

"Then I will have done no worse than Colley."

"Bravo," Hargood said. "That is the attitude. I will make it my business to see that you apply it consistently."

Beneath the flow of his discourse, Hargood's demolition of the pile of meat on his plate continued steadily. There was pace in Hargood's eating, in the swing of his knife, in the dip of his head as he raised a bloody piece of meat to his lips. Once begun, he sustained his momentum. Grange was a little slower, subject to occasional delays. Hargood paused before speaking:

"What troubles me most, I would say, is the smallpox inoculation."

"How so?"

"It is the unpredictability," Hargood's fork hovered before his mouth, "when applied to the mass. Fighting fire with fire is a dangerous business. We are at the early days. Applied to an entire population . . ."

"Yet surely you have enough spare souls in the balance to risk some experiments?"

"Silas, you are cruel enough to show up my reason. I cannot so easily dismiss the inoculations that were carried out here perhaps eight years ago when, as you no doubt recall, the parish churchwardens and overseers grew alarmed at the incidence of smallpox among the poor and voted for wholesale inoculations. Do you remember the score then, sir? Beckley inoculated some three hundred, of whom two died, Dolland about five hundred, of whom none died, Nike about three hundred, of whom eighteen died. Poor Nike must have used more contagious matter, but how was he to know?"

"It was unfortunate," Grange admitted. "As you say, it would be difficult to be constantly meeting the relations of the deceased, who would know little of the circumstances."

"Thank God the people here are like savages, and accept such things as part of the natural order. But because of that and other incidents, at this stage I prefer nature to undertake her own infections."

"Beneath that robust surface," Grange remarked, "do I detect a human doubt?"

Hargood leaned back and loosened his belt, the better to eat a second helping. "A human doubt? No. A practical opinion, merely. I will not play with fire while there is much material that one might accidentally set alight."

Grange nodded: "Jenner has written an *Inquiry into the Cause and Effects of the Variolae Vaccinae*."

"What is its import?"

"He argues that there are two different forms of the cowpox disease, only one of which protects against smallpox, and that many of the failures in application of the cowpox inoculation may thus be explained."

"He has tested his hypothesis?"

"An eight-year-old boy was inoculated with the matter from the cowpox vesicles on the hands of a milkmaid. A year later, the boy was inoculated for smallpox, but the disease did not follow."

"A beginning," Hargood admitted. "But we will need further tests."

"Indeed," Grange replied. "Though for myself I believe Dr. Jenner is on the right road."

Hargood became suddenly suspicious at the warmth of Grange's support. "This Jenner, he has received his degree from Edinburgh?"

"St. Andrews," Grange responded, then added with a certain satisfaction, "much the same thing."

5

"Another slice?" Hargood asked.

"I have had enough," Grange replied.

Hargood shrugged his shoulders and helped himself to several further thick layers of beef, but before committing himself to their demolition he leaned back.

"Silas, you think of me as a very rake of a fellow. Yet consider this. If in this world a man finds satisfaction and contentment, why should he leave its source? That is where I differ from your rake. Is it not normal to be imbued with tenderness toward her who brings him joy?"

This unexpected change of direction caused Grange to pause in his eating and consider his host briefly. He decided to wait before answering.

Hargood continued: "What is it that our rake lacks, at least in the expression? Tenderness, I would say. I ask myself, why does he not possess it? If there is some gentleness at his core, why should he hold back these emotions?"

"Hargood, I fail to see what you are driving at."

Hargood studied him dispassionately: "I am driving at you, sir."

"At me?"

"In you there is a terrible detachment. You are an idealist, to be sure. But, I ask myself, is that not the product of this detachment?"

"Do you make a statement or frame a question?"

"I have been in this world longer than you, and already I am at an age where one looks back and counts one's mistakes. If I search for sources of contentment, it is not in dominance, or in triumph, or in the expression of my will against others, but precisely in that tenderness which in a man is not thought important. Heaven's gold is kindness of heart."

"Hargood, you are the kindliest of men. But perhaps you will allow me time to find my way."

"What is a man?" Hargood asked, warming to his theme. "A mere accessory to the qualities of woman. It is woman who is the primary quantity, who is at the center of existence."

"Indeed?"

"That is what I say. What is man, then, compared to a woman—if not a child, a powerful child?"

"Hargood . . ."

"Think of it. Are there not more fine women than fine men?"

"Yes, I would believe so."

"Then why do you not take one up? Someone who is simple, and kind of heart?"

"Perhaps I will, in due course."

Raising his wineglass, and swilling the contents, Hargood addressed the room before him: "Yet the one to whom you direct your attentions is least gentle. You stalk our great lady like a tiger in the night."

"Hargood, I do not know of whom you speak . . ."

"The very things which cause me gravest doubt excite your curiosity."

"Of whom . . . ?"

"I speak of Mrs. Quill, as you are well aware."

"Mrs. Quill?"

"Mrs. Quill."

"She is an acquaintance, merely," Grange replied, "if I can be so bold as even to characterize her as such—an admired acquaintance."

"I have seen you two standing at parties in earnest discussion, your heads close together."

"She has a very fine intelligence. She inspires in me both admiration and curiosity."

"Mrs. Quill has all the qualities you claim. That is not in question. The question is your motive. I believe your curiosity will lead you to Hell, sir," Hargood commented without apparent animosity, indeed a certain amount of rough goodwill, as though Hell was merely a district, like Cheapside, which a gentleman should attempt to avoid.

"How may I deal with my curiosity," Grange asked, "except to allay it?"

"You will allay it, sir," Hargood said with considerable satisfaction, "and I will be King Nebuchadnezzar!"

Yet afterward, with a wink, Hargood raised up the five-branched candelabra, put his finger across his lips, and led Grange to the rear of the house by way of the hallway and a small corridor. Reaching the library, he unlocked the heavy oak door and pushed it from him. They stepped into a dark, airless room. As they advanced into it and the light from the flames picked up its surface details, so the contents became clearer. It was a private gallery, the gallery of a rich bachelor. On the walls were dozens of oil paintings, whose lacquered surfaces glinted sometimes in the light of the five flames. Of the paintings themselves, there were several attributes in common. They were all of the human figure, nearly all were female (except for a sprinkling of satyrs and cupids), and all were almost without exception in a state of near or absolute nakedness.

In the half-light Hargood chuckled. "I keep it locked from Mrs. Simmons." He advanced toward one painting of two shepherdesses and a dark Pan. "What do you think of this, for example?"

Grange paused, allowing his eyes to adjust. "A most inter-esting execution. I do feel that so much of art is due to its background. Paper glued to a more solid back, for example, is excellent. In certain paintings, paintings that are executed ac-cording to mood, no other material gives such transparency to browns or so much depth to blacks. I believe that this one must be upon such a background."

"You test my patience, Silas. Do you not like the scene?"

"Magnificent," Grange murmured. "A perfect technique. In Italy the white poplar was used as background, whereas in Flanders they use oak. There are some who say mahogany is preferred to oak, because it does not crack so much."

They moved on. "And this one?" Hargood asked.

"Who is the painter?"

"It is *The Three Graces* by François Boucher, copied," Hargood added hastily, "by a gifted young student of the Acad-emy."

"Exceptionally well achieved," Grange said, "though I do not entirely approve of the thickness of the varnish. In some places it has been applied in what the Italians call *impasto*."

"And here," Hargood said, moving on to another painting, "I have a genuine Montmorency."

"Indeed."

As Hargood moved, his forward motion imparted a breeze to the flames, which ducked and became small. When halted, the flames seemed to hesitate, gather themselves, and grow tall again. At each halt, Grange waited several seconds for this brighter radiance to deliver the image from the dark.

They were standing now in front of a single tall painting. It featured a cascade of nymphs, satyrs, and cherubs, a symphony of flesh. Yet the painting appeared oddly disembodied, as if it had no center, no point of contact. The female body was intimate, inviting the eyes toward its rotundities and hidden shadows, but the sheer numbers of figures in this case appeared to deflect the eye. It seemed to Grange that quantity had been preferred over quality. He did not say so to Hargood, though, who stood in wonder before the scale and breadth of execution.

Yet if there was a theme to the paintings before him, it was the interior mind of the male bachelor. It suggested a vista that was succulent, fleshy, and expressive. Painting after painting offered the richness of female flesh. To Grange it seemed that Hargood had his private harem, his herd of human dairy cows.

"What do you think?" Hargood asked.

"It is my observation that those which are painted on dark grounds last least well, whereas those with a light background preserve a miraculous freshness."

"And this one?" Hargood continued to advance.

Three women in an interior, one reclining, another standing, while a third—no doubt a maid or handmaiden, one of the few fully dressed females in the room—stood behind her, fitting stays.

"When I am old," Hargood commented, in the flickering light, "and incapable of physical satisfaction, I will stagger here to remember what I once enjoyed."

"I say it is a good investment," Grange said, "though I suspect your retirement is a long time coming."

"A most apposite remark." Hargood moved onward in the darkness, absorbed in contemplation. "Perhaps I perceive some sense in you at last."

They moved in due course to the door.

"You came by horse?" Hargood asked.

"I walked. I enjoy the night air."

"I hope you do not meet a ghost or spirit."

"You believe in ghosts?" Grange asked.

Hargood opened the door. The night air chilled Grange's back; despite midsummer mists, there was a clear view of the sky. He intended to walk by cool starlight along the foreshore.

"To this extent," Hargood said. "Certain of our friends are strong presences, I think you will agree. When they depart this world, they leave an absence that is no less powerful."

"And so?"

"What is a ghost," Hargood said grandly, "except an intense absence?"

"But is this absence outside us, Hargood? Is it something concrete? Or is it a sensation inside us, like the memory of a lost arm?"

"Whether it is inside or outside, I do not care. It is experienced. It is felt. That is sufficient. Whose arm did you remove, by the way? It sounds to me as though you have removed your own."

"My patient is a Mr. Swann. Perhaps I feel a certain sympathy."

"Sympathy!" Hargood growled. "A doctor cannot afford sympathy. It impedes his duties. Damn me. Sympathy is a mechanism for making two people unhappy where only one was unhappy before."

The candleflames flickered in the night air, almost died, revived. In his absorption with the mechanics of light, Grange was aware that the first extensive use of illuminating gas was already under way in Redruth, in Cornwall. Its inventor, William Murdock, had recently lighted his home with it. It would be slow in arriving, though Hargood had already spoken of utilizing it to light his own house, if he could only find a supply of gas. Now Hargood said:

"I will walk with you a few steps. I always enjoy your visits so. Tell me, is there anything on which we are inclined to agree?"

There was a trace of anxiousness in Hargood's voice, and Grange was concerned to reassure him.

"I believe there is nothing," Grange replied.

"I am fearful that we will find something upon which we shall, and then our friendship will dissolve."

"Every effort must be made to ensure that it does not happen."

"We speak of opposites, sir. Yet out of the purest flame comes the deepest lampblack." Hargood halted at the periphery of light from the hallway lamp. "I bid you a final adieu."

"Good night," Grange said. He put on his hat, waved once, and started into the night, following the line of the paving stones. His path led him across the field toward the gate and roadway. The effects of the wine made him feel light. If nothing else, he was grateful to Hargood for allaying a certain morbidity.

6

*F*or all his good cheer at Hargood's, he slept uneasily that night. Some agitation of the mind brought him awake before dawn, and he lay in his bed, his open eyes pressed against the solid darkness, trying to recall the obscure and perplexing shape of a dream. On other nights, suffering from insomnia, he would light a candle and read a text from Aristotle, or the philosophy of David Hume, which would demand his close attention and calm his mind through concentration. Mrs. Thompson would knock on his door to rouse him and find him, the door open to gain a draft in the hot summer weather, lying forward over the desk, having achieved sleep at last.

This morning he felt stronger agitation than could be easily calmed by reading, and a desire to walk off some of the muzziness of Hargood's wine. When the first trace of dawn could be seen in the window frame, he rose, put on trousers and shirt, stockings and walking shoes, and crept downward through the house in order not to wake Mrs. Thompson.

Outside, in the street, he closed the door quietly and lowered the latch. Hardly a dog stirred. Looking east, early light glowed above the brow of Walhampton Hill. Only the brief neighing and quick stutter of hooves could be heard, from the horses in the ostlery being readied for the early morning Telegraph coach to Southampton. He walked down the hill toward the river, crossed the bridge, nodding to the drowsing toll attendant. On Walhampton's shore, he halted and peered out across the slowly increasing light to the rim of water meadows and estuaries that stretched toward the Isle of Wight.

More than all the other birds, Grange loved the great gray herons that inhabited the marshes, for their solitariness, their silence, their casual grace as they swam upward into the air. He loved them too for the calm, recondite heartbeat of their wings when agitated. In surveying them, their silence moved him to remark on his own solitude, and perhaps therein lay an identity of interest, or at least of common form. When disturbed, they seemed to move upward into the thinner medium as calmly as thought, grasping the air in their big wings like hands. Above all he loved the shapes into which they transposed in the gray above him. Sometimes they drew their wings in close to the thin body, seeming as heavy as a piece of falling masonry; or they spread their wings wide, resembling instead some great, cold archangel.

He took to watching them whenever he could, either in

the early mornings or at dusk when his visitations were over, and returned home vaguely disappointed if he had not seen at least one. Attempting without success to capture some element of their grace, he had written a few lines in his diary:

> *Chaste, dissolving driftwood,*
> *Decaying bait in mouth of air,*
> *With two wingbeats spread a lake.*

But he could get no further than a sensory impression obtained by these brief phrases, which in their turn led nowhere. He could not form a poem, and this fragment, the sum of his observations, would have to stand for him.

When he returned, there was a sign of traffic on the footpaths surrounding the town. Laborers walked alone, or in silent twos and threes, through the fields. A gang of men in a cart were drawn by two heavy horses toward the Pylewell salt furnace, where a dark plume was already rising above the squat building on the foreshore.

Leaving the house that morning, he had unbolted the door and left it on the latch so that he could enter quietly, without calling the attention of his housekeeper. Mrs. Thompson could be heard in the kitchen, above the thin whistle of the boiling kettle. A series of light thuds and the creak of a heavy metal hinge indicated that she was piling extra logs into the stove. He heard her pause in her activity as he walked up the stairs, and knew that she was listening to his comings and goings with her sharp ears.

In his bedroom, a flask of heated water had been placed by Mrs. Thompson on the sideboard beside the metal basin at which he shaved. She would know for certain that he had risen early that morning to take the air. Their relationship was such that he took this interest for granted. It was part of her character. Since her husband had died some six years previously of wasting disease, the entire force of her character had been directed, by a kind of natural displacement, into her work. Since he and his well-being were effectively the object of that work, he had accepted, a little grudgingly at first, the legitimacy of her interest in his own affairs. He suspected that, like many strong women who had been bereaved, in some part of her character she blamed herself for the loss of her husband, and would strive to see that no harm came to her employer, who was now the primary focus of her concern.

Behind the bedroom door he removed his shirt to shave, poured warm water into a basin, and when he had finished he flung a few handfuls of cold water over his face from a second pitcher. Refreshed, having dressed and brushed his hair, he descended to the hall where Mrs. Thompson had set out a table and a plate with several slices of cold roast pork. It was his own belief that the popular diet was too great in its volume of meat. The richer classes subsisted primarily on beef, the less well off on mutton, the artisans and laborers on pork, supplemented by pigeons, ducks, and poultry. Vegetables and fruit, whose nutritional value was considered to be lacking, were the final prerogative for the unfortunate and those too destitute to afford meat. In their eating habits, the various classes expressed themselves as a hierarchy of carnivores.

Mrs. Thompson followed a traditional line. She held to the view that the more meat that was eaten, the better. Accordingly, she was never happier than on those occasions when Grange ate well. It was one of a number of areas of small skirmish between them, in that no-man's-land between his desire for a measure of independence and her direct concern, in which they had agreed to differ, though their differences were carefully drawn and assiduously patrolled.

That morning his own appetite, generally somewhat unreliable, had been given an edge by the walk, and he sat down thoughtfully to demolish what had been set on his plate. Although on this rare occasion he could easily have consumed the entire contents, he nevertheless left one slice uneaten, as an indication of his own beliefs in sobriety, and as a signal to

Mrs. Thompson that he maintained at least a token guard over the fine line of his private determination.

For her part Mrs. Thompson, patrolling her own outposts, lingered for a second longer than was necessary over the remaining slice before raising the plate and disappearing without comment to the kitchen.

7

*I*t was not absolutely certain when Mrs. Celia Quill had arrived, because she was calm and without pretensions, and the house which she had chosen, the Gaskills, was in a discreet location drawn back from the thoroughfare, in the quiet lanes that spread thinly on top of the hill at Walhampton. Yet Mrs. Quill had taken up her residence with all the quiet glory of one from the better society of London. A few weeks after her move, once she had settled in, several of the local women of good family had called upon her and emerged impressed, if not slightly awed, by her good taste, humility, and the atmosphere of good breeding which both she and her residence distilled. A widow, she was a handsome woman of some forty years or so, well preserved. She dressed quietly, but her clothes set off her face and her regal bearing. It was said that she had two daughters who were themselves married, one of whom lived not far away in Winchester.

A widow may be an awkward guest at a dinner table, but her tact and consideration soon endeared Mrs. Quill to her neighbors, and those who took to visiting her also began inviting her to their own houses. By the end of two seasons, she was an accepted part of the small society and its surrounds. Sir Harry Burrard Neale, their member of Parliament, had taken to inviting her for dinner at the behest of his wife. Though some considered her cool, she could listen with calm solicitude to those who were distressed, or who sought her advice (as several increasingly did), and those who did discovered her suggestions were both impartial and practical. They found, little by little, that at the root of her fine manners there appeared to be an extraordinary goodness.

Grange had lived in Lymington some twelve years, nearly thirteen, establishing his precarious foothold and slowly beginning to think himself part of a community. She had alighted only three years before, and was a relative newcomer. But already her reputation had eclipsed those who had been there more years, and were longer on the social scene. They said she read books diligently, and sometimes those wives or their relations who approached her to discuss local matters were surprised at her knowledge of wider aspects, and the unobtrusive but confident manner in which she dispensed her wisdom.

It was the calmness of her arrival that surprised him. It seemed that with uncanny speed she now appeared indispensable to society. She had contributed unstintingly to the charity of the parish. No cause, however humble, was beneath her concern. She made woolen garments with her own hands for the poorhouse, contributing some £15 a year for the coffers of the same. In this endeavor not only did a number of her friends follow her example, but began to form a society for the poor and fallen.

In the course of his limited social life, Grange had met her several times. The first was at the Sopers' house, near Lepe, at a celebration of the Reverend Soper's daughter's wedding. They had come face to face in the hallway. He had meant merely to introduce himself, but she had granted him instead a half hour of her conversation, during which he felt himself continually the subject of her calm gray eyes, and came under the influence of a mind that was quiet but of extraordinary breadth. She asked him why he had traveled to Scotland to take his medical degree. He expounded to her his admiration for the Scottish enlighteners David Hume and Adam Smith, whose precepts he admitted he did not fully understand, though he felt sufficiently acquainted with their thought to believe that Edinburgh was the scene of the greatest achievement in Europe. She smiled, but did not laugh, when he told her he believed the Royal College of Physicians of Edinburgh was the most radical and forward-looking of societies. He began to bubble, to tell her of his gratitude to Dr. Hargood, who had taken him under his wing and helped him to establish himself, and that however much Hargood might tease him about his "northern alignment," being himself a fellow of the Royal College of Physicians, Grange himself believed there was much that could be done, not least in the matter of cleanliness, but also the use of antiseptics and the necessity of extreme care not to transfer traces of cadaverous matter on the physician's hands. She calmly allowed him to talk, encouraging him with well-placed questions if he hesitated, even though he wished to hear her views more than his own.

On the several other occasions they had met, she had been equally generous with her time. Perhaps they both sensed, as if by some common intuition, that it was now appropriate to cement their social relations. Grange considered this prospect with both optimism and trepidation now as he walked down the High Street and across the tollbridge to Walhampton. It was merely one of Hargood's several good offices that Grange had been issued a pass by the borough so that, if he was on foot, he might proceed across the bridge without paying a toll, though he was obliged when on horseback to contribute one and a half pence per crossing. The bridge was primarily a causeway across a broad section of the river, with a bridge on the Walhampton side to allow the free flow of the current. Downstream, on the banks of the Walhampton water, lay flat-bottomed salt barges, drawn up like seals, a caulk or stopper opened to let out the rainwater that would otherwise collect in the bilges. On the Lymington side of the river the highest building on the foreshore was a tidal mill, with a pool that was used to drive the great waterwheel.

Having crossed the tollbridge, to reach Mrs. Quill's house it was necessary to walk for a hundred yards or so along the road that wound along the Walhampton foreshore, then follow a footpath up through a copse of birch, elm, and spruce trees, until you arrived at the top of the hill. There you swung right, into Barrows Lane, and came almost by chance upon the secluded entrance.

8

A formal garden hid the house from the roadway. Once
inside the gate, a high yew hedge, supplemented by a line of
palings, reduced further the view of the house so that, walking
along the brick path that led through the garden, the residence
itself was not quite visible. Only its tall chimneys gave a clue
to its presence behind a further line of elms. He glanced into
a quadrangle of carefully paved stones lined with flower beds;

phlox, marigold, buttercup. A second pathway followed the curve of yew hedge, along which he began to walk.

Rounding the final hedge, the house came into view, set back in its own lawns, a handsome red-bricked building with classical proportions in doors and windows. It faced directly south, toward the Isle of Wight, but the combination of sloping ground to the right and its own position on a rise raised its purview above the immediate surrounds of Walhampton, and addressed itself beyond the undershore to the Solent waters and the gold line of cliffs opposite Hurst Castle. Once it had belonged to a sea captain grown rich on the salt trade, who had built it with the intention of observing sea traffic entering and leaving through the Hurst narrows. Now the observation post which he had kept on the first floor had been dismantled, and Mrs. Quill merely enjoyed the magnificent sea views.

Approaching the house itself, Grange glanced around the garden. Close by the house were several shrubs and bushes, a peach tree neatly pinned against the south wall. It was a day of tepid sunlight and overcast cloud. His shoes grated on the pebbles as he walked toward the front door.

He raised and lowered the door knocker, then stood back. In the interval, as if in compensation for the indifference of the light, birds and insects sang without cease. Footsteps approached from inside, a shadow moved under the doorway; a bolt was drawn and the door was opened. It was too light to see immediately inside, but out of the placid interior Mrs. Quill's unmistakable voice said warmly: "Dr. Grange. How good to see you."

Unable to focus, Grange gave the gloom of the doorway the benefit of a cautious smile, nodded a careful bow, and stepped forward out of the sunlight. For a short while his eyes were filled with darkness. It took several further seconds to make the adjustment from sunlit exterior to shady interior. As part of this adjustment, Mrs. Quill emerged out of the darkness of interior shadow, her fine face smiling, as she studied him across the small space of the hall.

. . .

"You seem well," his hostess said. Before Grange could respond, however, she turned and led the way down a corridor, so that he followed the silent grace of her back in the gloom, past a wall clock and several high hall cupboards, emerging suddenly into the lighter atmosphere of the drawing room. She halted and turned to face him. "Please be seated, sir."

The room was perhaps twenty feet square, lit from the south by three tall windows. Grange had the habit of sweeping an arm behind to gather his coattails around his side, so that they were not crushed beneath him, and sat down quietly in the high-backed chair she had indicated. Mrs. Quill continued to stand, and for several moments he wondered what this might mean. A sense of decorum prevented Grange from speaking. At the same time Mrs. Quill appeared content to prolong the silence, so that Grange's smile slowly faded as the seconds passed. While the outer form of his face settled, his mind became more thoughtful.

Yet Mrs. Quill moved several more times before she spoke. The first was a slight turn of her head to the right, the second a graceful shift of her body to follow. Now she turned again and was standing in profile, looking out of the window toward the Solent. Having taken her position, she pivoted her face to glance at him, and he thought at last she might begin to speak, but again she turned away as if to consider the view. He had the impression that he should remain quiet, that she was gathering her resources.

Mrs. Quill said calmly, "I thank you for attending my request."

It was formal, and yet some heightened sense gave rise to the feeling that what she was about to disclose deserved this formality.

She began: "I ask that you may be patient with me. Recommended as you are by many, sir, I do not yet know you well. On those occasions that we met, circumstances allowed a fleeting exchange."

Grange nodded once, briefly. But Mrs. Quill seemed not to have noticed, for she resumed:

"Except on such occasions as we have spoken, I do not

know what you think on this or that subject. It is, I suppose, part of our condition. What you think is your own affair. I intend to risk today my own thoughts in the hope that I may convey, if nothing else, an attitude with which I hope you may agree. And if, sir, you agree, then upon agreed principle we may perhaps act."

Grange said, "It is my honor to be addressed by you."

Mrs. Quill smiled.

"I am remiss, sir. I should have offered you a drink. Will you take a cordial?"

Grange waved a hand. "No thank you, madam."

Mrs. Quill turned away and directed her gaze once again through the window. "You sit so silent I am emboldened to think you patient. For my sermon, sir, I would say this. We know our state of man. His wishes are made known, his activities engaged, his triumphs trumpeted abroad. Instead, I wish to speak of woman." She paused for fully several seconds, visibly gathering herself, but by now he had become almost used to these sentences, this mode of speech, and was determined to let her proceed without either encouragement or interruption.

"When I was young, I was so nervous of my condition, I did nothing. But inside I waited, waited for my fate. What that fate might be I did not know. Waiting for what one does not know is waiting long. I waited, as I say. And what happened then was not the fruit of waiting. I was, I suppose, distracted. A good gentleman asked me to be his wife. I had waited long for something, and though this were not the outcome I sought, I accepted—the alternative being further waiting."

Poised, the curve of her arm, her hand resting on the sill, although her speech was calm, he noticed with some surprise she was taking deep breaths, as if it cost her something to formulate her thoughts.

"We were married, we lived together. We were not unhappy. We mated, sir, and produced two children. Both are grown and recently departed into marriage. My husband died five years ago, of age and complications. That good man I laid to rest. Some further time passed. Having mourned, I thought again about my fate. I hope I do not bore you?"

Startled, Grange said: "You do not, madam. I am here and full of silence."

"Then I will test your patience further. I must speak now most freely. But first I would ask you this. If what I say does not agree with you, then you must tell me. And if we speak no more, you must assure me that you will not mention our discussion to another living soul. Do I have your assurance?"

"You have it," Grange answered. "Not to a living soul."

She appeared satisfied with his confirmation, yet paused again, as if gathering her resources.

"Before I begin, I am affixed with the notion that what I tell appears shameful. It is not shameful to me. Perhaps in that I am afflicted. Since the views of men are various, I say again, sir, that if what I say distresses, or annoys, or stands in the way of our continued understanding, I will not hold it against you if you interrupt me, and after I have given you a cordial, depart hence with our friendship unaltered and maintained."

"Your speech intrigues me, madam. Please continue."

Mrs. Quill half smiled: "Being full of silence, sir, you listen well."

He nodded politely. A fly moved across the perspective, struck the glass windowpane, and was deflected out of his direct sight. Mrs. Quill's breathing seemed to have settled.

"I spoke to you of waiting. Waiting for an outcome. That was my lot. It is the lot of women. We wait, sir, most of us, for what we do not know. We are conditioned thus by waiting, until waiting itself becomes our condition. Our souls are suspended. We conduct our lives. We engage in movement, but inside we are silent."

"All souls are lonely, madam," suggested Grange tentatively, "though women may feel it most."

She paused briefly, and then continued:

"Now I come to that which requires my courage to speak of. I speak, sir, of myself, and say that one day I was woken, but I shall endeavor to explain the meaning of that word. It happened well into my life, when I had waited so long I had forgotten I was waiting. In my widowhood, several years after my husband's death, I had done all that I could to repair his loss and settle into my existence. My two children, both girls, were by then married. I returned to my house one day and heard a small sound upstairs; hardly a sound, perhaps merely a disturbance in my ear. It was late afternoon. I had been out walking. Returning, I had entered quietly. My maid had departed that day to see her family, and my good cook was out purchasing provisions. There was no one in my household that I knew of. Returning, I thought I should rest for a little.

"I waited further. No sound came. I thought the small commotion I had heard upstairs was an animal perhaps—a wainscot mouse, nothing more. Reassured that the house was empty, I took off my cloak and hung it in the hall. I entered the sitting room where you sit now, and prepared to sit in that very chair, when I heard again a small commotion.

"In curiosity more than trepidation, I advanced up the stairs, one by one in my soft shoes, until I reached the floor above. I waited and I heard no further. Perhaps I should have returned. It was only some unaccustomed certainty, some strangeness of fancy that kept me there. I waited as if I knew what I were waiting for. The sound came again, hardly a sound at all, a scratch, then it was silent.

"I said I was not frightened. No, I was like some cat that prowls a roof. I advanced down the corridor as lightly as I could, avoiding any board that creaked until, at the end of the corridor, I came to a room whose interior I suspected. The door was partly ajar. It was a room I used to store old clothes and some worthless trinkets, more out of sentiment than anything else. I peered round the door.

"In the interior of the room there was a great distress of clothing that had been taken from drawers and chests. I observed that the window was open. At first I thought the intruder had left, and the open window was evidence of his escape. About to advance into the room I heard, again, that noise, and turning my vision to the right, to the furthest corner of the room, I spied him. The perpetrator of this outrage was even then, in a manner both swift and quiet, opening another drawer to be rifled.

"You may think again I should have been alarmed. Yet I was more curious than fearful. For in that moment I perceived several things. Firstly, the perpetrator seemed no great criminal or malcontent. He was small and ragged—a man, but in a boy's frame from starvation. His hair was uncut. His sleeves had been slit and his arms were brown from sun and dirt. One bare calf protruded from ragged breeches. He had no footwear. This was a figure commanding pity more than rage. At that stage in my stalk of him, I wished merely to affright, to send him scurrying through the window like some monkey, his pockets empty and terror in his soul. He faced away from me and now, unaware of my presence, was hauling out clothes in abandon. But a strange thought possessed me. Watching his endeavors, I was struck by a hard curiosity to see his face, to look into the eyes of one such as he.

"It was perhaps a dangerous notion, but I was gripped, commanded by it. I say I felt no fear. While he pulled fresh drawers and threw the contents down beside his ragged feet, I slipped into the room behind him, and moved as soft as foot would allow toward the window, intending to cut off his retreat. I had but reached the other side before my shadow must have affected the light sufficiently to alarm him of some other presence, for he whirled round, and saw me standing silent, watching him.

"He was not handsome in any manner, one of those stray scraps who are neither man nor boy, but hover between the ages of fourteen and forty. His face was caked with dirt. I saw his eyes peer at me like a frightened animal. Then his glance moved rapidly toward the window from which I had cut off easy retreat, then again toward the open door. I perceived that he was deciding whether to rush past me or flee through the door to seek an outlet somewhere else. Something rose in me. I said, 'I will let you go.'

"He looked at me as if a statue had spoken, and began to shake and quiver, as if what I had suggested was so fearful and full of foreboding that he would rush that very moment through the door. I knew I was on the point of losing him, this scrap that excited my curiosity. That was when, sir, I acted most shamelessly of all. I said, 'I have need of you before you go.'

"He looked at me with no less agitation. On the contrary, he seemed about to spring to his escape . . . That was when, attempting not to alarm him but at the same time to distract him from sudden flight, I reached down with my hands most carefully and, before his very eyes, I . . . raised my dress . . ."

Mrs. Quill faced away, staring through the window at the light on the water. Grange's face was frozen with listening. Even the light, the very air, seemed still.

"If I could tell you that what I desired was not lasciviousness, you would, sir, not believe me. I desired to prolong his stay, and such was my curiosity that I knew only one thing that perhaps would hold him. Sir, I expect no mercy in your thoughts for thus revealing what I felt. For it led, as I will tell you, to the same thing.

"I raised my dress, and I saw his eyes move at last from the two escapes of window and door which until now had formed his whole world. I raised my dress, sir, like a curtain on a stage. And when I stood there, I saw a changed expression that vied with his terror. I will halt in these inspections, my modesty being gone. I halt for no other reason than that of economy. You may guess what happened. He was distracted. I do not know for how long, for a few minutes or the best part of an hour. When the time, short or long, was over, I felt for the first time that joy which I had denied myself for my whole life. I could have sung."

Grange felt that he might never move again, as if the world itself was balanced on the single, perfect point of his astonishment. Yet one part of him was alive, one tiny cog of consciousness which said, "Be still and it will be revealed." He heard the sound of breathing, deep, regular, his own. But it was Mrs. Quill's voice which summoned him again:

"Now, sir, you are truly full of silence. Speak. Say I am shameless. Make your position known."

9

*F*or several seconds Grange could not speak. Light seemed to fill the room. As if by some act of displacement, he examined through the window behind her the distant prospect, and was provoked to wonder, how can the roof and floor of the earth ever meet, rising off the water like a luminous field?

His astonishment, if it did not fade, was static and could be put aside. Now, as if his life had been given back to him, he breathed in, composed himself, stood up, turned directly toward her. It seemed to him, standing there, that little in life is certain. He did not know what precisely caused him to speak as he now did, as if a sense of recklessness had invaded his soul, a courage sympathetic to hers.

"Madam, you are very fine to address me thus." He halted briefly, as though listening to his own words, and then continued: "What I perceive is not shamelessness but courage. What you speak of is not subject for remorse. You waited, and your waiting brought you fate—in unexpected form. There is no harm in that."

She gazed out through the window, unmoving, so he continued:

"You were frightened to speak, so let me now speak for you. You found that what you sought was here, that what you did so freely, freed you. You are lucky, madam, for such joy touches precious few. And having found that joy, you expected remorse. If your behavior shocked the mind which is conditioned, what shocked you more is that after the remittance of that joy you felt no anguish. None whatsoever. A happiness assailed you, both savage and sublime. I say it was this feeling that shocked you more than what you did, though in my terms that sense of emotion is innocent and pure enough."

The storm inside him seemed to subside a little. He caught his breath, and persevered: "It was not the act itself, but lack of grievous consequence that so frightened you. You should have been affected by afterthought. You should have punished yourself. But on the contrary, what you felt was joy, compounding your own sin. Tell me, madam, I am right? You felt no remorse?"

"Not a trace, sir."

Grange nodded once to himself. He had delivered his elegy to her in a state of profoundest agitation. Now the simple speaking of it seemed to calm him. She was still facing away. He returned to his chair and sat down.

"I apologize for talking in your name, for stealing your discretion."

"Do not apologize."

For several seconds he was silent, watching her back, her neck, the concentration of her poise. "If that is what you asked me here to tell me, madam, I am privileged. I promise you no one shall know a word of what you spoke. More than anything, I admire courage. That is what I have learned. Courage and clear-mindedness are the greatest virtues. If you know what brings you joy, then you are lucky. Blessed are they who reach out and seize their happiness."

Mrs. Quill, swinging to face him, turned upon him now a smile of magnificent but temporary radiance. Then, as if gathering her thoughts, she turned away to the distant view again, appeared to compose herself, and said:

"I thank you for what you have to say. You are most kind and civil. And if that were all, I would thank you again for your patience. But my experience is compounded by further thought. For now, encouraged by you, I will continue. You see, sir, I not only felt no remorse, but wished indeed to perpetuate my condition. I was worried by my visitor's appearance. He looked fragile, sickly pale. One day someone not as well disposed as I would catch him in the act of theft and he would lose a hand, or to a penal colony would be sent. I own that afterward I held on to him, like a drowning person a piece of driftwood. I heard my cook come into the kitchen below. My unexpected visitor was alarmed, alarmed as any animal. I tried to calm him. I said I was the mistress of the house, and the cook would not venture these stairs unless called expressly. I took some coins from a small purse on my dress—a trifle for me but enough for a wainscot mouse to live on for a week— and I gave it to him.

"And, sir, in this my sin was compounded. For I realized I had no shame deeper than regret at not seeing him again. So, shameless, I said he should visit me as he would wish. I was both coy and mischievous. I told him that if he called the same time next week, there would be no one waiting but myself. And in the meantime, I did beg him not to steal. For if he were to return, I could provision him sufficiently to keep without theft until our next meeting . . . I think he thought me mad

. . . Now I have told you all. Admit, sir, you are shocked."

"Madam, I apologized to you for stealing your thoughts. Now, be not so quick with mine. What I hear is music. A sweet tale. Where neither was happy, two are happy now, albeit briefly. I am a rationalist. If God's against that, I am against God."

A trace of amusement entered the expression of her face, compounded by relief. Yet she appeared determined on her course.

"There is no need to blaspheme on my account, sir. Your agreement is welcome enough. If you will have patience with me, I shall speak of this further. What I experienced was not love, but physical awakening. I loved my husband dutifully, but I did not experience that happiness which makes the soul sing. What I have to ask you now will test your patience finally."

"I listen, madam, as yet untested."

"So, I shall continue. My own happiness was discovered by chance. Yet I have two daughters in the world who will be subject to the same cruel fate as I before my waking. I know that they too wait. They are married as I was. Yet they too may die in that state which I call sleeping, having never woken. I think of others also, of all the fine and worthy women I have known who will continue sleeping . . ."

"Madam . . ."

"Those who have woken are those who have reached out and seized their fate, who have brushed the other world aside like beasts who know their instincts . . ."

"It was always the way . . ."

"They are the more selfish, the least good. Beside these skirmishers and sinners stand those women who have sacrificed themselves to duty, husband, children, home. Having given so much of themselves, sir, it is these, rather than the mistresses and strumpets, who should by rights be wakened."

Grange laughed softly to himself in recognition of a melancholy fact.

"Madam, you know our system better than I. It is monstrously unfair. But what is not, in life?"

"Sir, that is where we differ. I do not accept that if it is so, it should be so."

"Neither do I. But even thus, it is so."

"Then," Mrs. Quill said firmly, "one day perhaps we will talk again how it might be changed."

"Madam"—Grange spoke with a certain irony—"I did not perceive in your courage until now the sin of agitation against the natural order."

"I do not agitate, sir, or speak on a box. I am of a private disposition. I merely think of putting into practice what I think. In which I need assistance and close company."

"How so?"

"If one man could bring a brief delight to certain women, he could waken the sleeping."

Grange laughed again, half afraid, borne along by reason, yet resisting out of duty, like a brakeman on a coach. "Madam, there are those that do. They are called rakes."

"I do not speak of rakes, sir, who are inclined to regard women as trinkets to be collected, to have their reputations ruined, to be talked about with other men. A woman would be a fool to have to do with such."

"What do you speak of, then? Or who?"

"I speak of one whose discretion is the true guide of his action, whose mind is pure in its intent to please, who does not conquer in order to despoil."

"If such a man could be found, assuming that he could, how could he reach those deserving? They are armored in their virtue. They would reject him, distinguishing him no doubt as a rake. The fact is, madam, those very women who are most deserving are least accessible."

Mrs. Quill, facing away, did not appear to move, but he sensed something had changed, that she too now smiled to herself.

"You think constructively at last. To a man on his own, yes, what you say is true. If a woman were to guide him, less so."

Grange paused briefly, a part of his mind saying, This is absurd; this is an hypothesis. But he was never one unwilling to pursue a point of logic.

"Let us say that you found such a man. You would . . . help him?"

"Oh, I would help him with all my heart, sir."

"And who is this knight so courteous and saintly? I do not think I have met him or his kind yet."

"Now I know you jest, sir. You know whom I mean."

Grange experienced again the sensation of agitation rising like water. But something, a sense of her seriousness, prevented him laughing outright. He would bring an end to these proceedings, not precipitately but by careful application of the brake. Yet some part of the exhilaration was still with him.

"I am most flattered that you should even think of me thus. But"—he paused, choosing his words carefully, proceeding step by step—"I too have my boundaries, my small reputation, that I should not put aside, since it brings the confidence of others. My life is based on my discretion. I live in this life, in society, as you do, madam. My reputation is not as fine as yours, but it suits my purposes to maintain it."

"Do not be so fearful, sir. And so might it continue. If you were to agree, you would not be breaking any rules that I would know. You would not be exploiting the fairer sex, but helping them in their enlightenment. Where's the need of guilty conscience?"

"The need of guilty conscience? I need a clear conscience, madam, in order to perform my small function in this world."

"And that is exactly why you are most suitable. That is what you would maintain."

"We have covered much ground. It is wonderful to meet one such as you who thinks so clearly. But hearing you, I think the height of clarity may be as dangerous as any other height."

"Nothing is without danger, sir, including marriage and childbirth. Perhaps in what is necessary we women are less fearful of a fall."

"I grant you that."

"I see I have proceeded too far. I most earnestly thank you for your attentions, for your patience and kind comments. I have no doubt but that you are the man I seek, whether you agree or not. Having made my petition, I can do no more. Let us cease our discussion of these matters. May I offer you a cordial?"

"You may indeed," Grange replied. The nightmare and the dream receded. "It is a pleasure to be party to your hospitality."

10

Waking the following dawn it was not Swann's scream which caused Grange to lie shivering, but the sound of a lopped arm hitting the iron dish, the terrible flat sound of death, which is lack of animation. He thought of this over and over again; *lop-arm*, *deadweight*, *flatdish;* the fat and heavy sound of termination, the separation of the living from the dead. His anguish was physical rather than mental. He was aware, at a certain level, that his situation was relative. He could have been a ship's surgeon, with the floors painted red to hide the blood, forced during action perhaps to perform amputation after amputation while the groans of wretched men became a single chorus. He at least was not forced to spread sand on his floors to prevent himself slipping on the blood and gore from severed limbs. And yet a single scream pierced the silence more sharply, like a hard chisel, drove itself into the nervous system, remained there, bringing out its own echoes in dreams and recollection.

He lay thinking. The cotton sheets on which he slept were clean but rough. In the half-light they seemed to produce a faint effulgence or luminosity, like light rising from water. When he fell asleep again, the scream seemed to follow him at a distance, and when he woke once more it was full morning.

A cotton shirt, waistcoat, knee breeches. His hair was awry and he swept it back over his forehead with a brush whose back was whalebone. Cut short, it brushed more easily. Long hair was no longer fashionable in society, though it was often seen in the older drovers and swineherds who came into the town from the outlying New Forest. In the little reflecting glass, corners of hair stood proud over the ears.

Satisfied that he had met the requirements, Grange pulled on his long calfskin boots and walked out to the staircase, where he smelled the heartening aromas of breakfast cooking in Mrs. Thompson's kitchen.

So began a day like other days, which at the same time was unlike other days because a certain aspect of contemplation sat at the back of his mind. Though he performed his functions with reasonable aptitude and sufficient will, some aspect of him was not yet present. The feeling persisted through the morning, as if a part of him were still sleeping, and in the afternoon during which time he made his rounds and visited his patients. It was as if he was waiting for the day to disperse.

. . .

That evening, sitting at the head of his dining table, alone, immersed in private silence, Grange continued his waiting. The door had been left open to aerate the house. A calm dusk breeze ruffled the tablecloth, causing the hanging flaps to ripple like becalmed sails. Though there was still light enough to see, Mrs. Thompson had lit the candles on the table and placed glass shades over them to protect from the breeze. Even so the flames, encased by glass, moved nervously.

Around him, the large empty spaces echoed. He ate his soup contemplatively, with perhaps a little more noise than in polite company. Occasionally he paused, overcome by thought. Mrs. Thompson drifted solidly about the periphery, carrying plates or pans, replacing washed linen in the kitchen drawers. He finished the soup, tilting the plate toward him to form a final pool that his spoon could excavate. Belching softly, he broke with his hands the heavy brown bread that Mrs. Thompson had put out on a sideplate and with thick pieces scooped up the remainder of the soup.

When he had finished and put his plate aside, with a sigh of linen skirts Mrs. Thompson entered to change his course.

"Thank you." He leaned back in his chair while she cleared other plates away.

"Would you say most women are happy, Mrs. Thompson?"

A plate in each hand, as if weighing them like justice, Mrs. Thompson was suitably startled. "Happy, sir?"

"Would you say," Grange pursued, "that their souls sing?"

Mrs. Thompson swallowed briefly, arrested.

"If I knew what you meant, sir, I believe I might be able to answer you."

Folding his hands in front of him, Grange responded calmly, "If I knew what I meant, Mrs. Thompson, I'm not sure I would ask."

Mrs. Thompson glanced at him as if he were behaving strangely—as indeed he was—and returned to the kitchen. Not long afterward she entered again with a plate of lamb. Grange began his second course, slicing several pieces of lamb with a carving knife and transferring them by fork onto a side plate. It was something he enjoyed, an expression and display of his skill. But once this aptitude was expressed, he took up his knife and fork without much relish and continued to eat slowly for a short while, with a certain lack of interest. After a few more mouthfuls he put his food aside and commented, loud enough for Mrs. Thompson to hear:

"I'm not hungry."

Mrs. Thompson reappeared from the kitchen, a brisk cloud. "You're not sickening for something, are you, sir?"

Grange avoided answering, dabbing his mouth with the corner of the tablecloth. He held out toward her, with the courtesy of a brief nod, his half-filled and unwanted plate. She took it without question but, standing in front of him, bore down on him with her enquiring eyes.

Still musing, he pushed his chair back, rose to his feet, nodding once more to her to signal his departure. She took a step aside, on her trim ankles, to let him pass. She watched him as he walked toward the hallway, pausing only to lift one of the candles from the sideboard and carry it with him up the staircase to his study.

Arriving at his sanctum, Grange sat down, placing the candle on his desk. He paused for a few seconds to assemble his thoughts, then drew a blank page toward him. Taking a plume, he dipped it in ink and began to write, enunciating the words carefully as he moved the pen.

Dear Mrs. Quill,

I thank you for your invitation to visit you, and for the kindness of your hospitality.

For myself, I have no doubts that what you have said, with such eloquence, about the role of the fairer sex is true. Since, in my modest way, I try to follow truth, at least in the first and most incomplete understanding of it, I should like to listen further to what you say.

Perhaps you think I am unworthy to be further audience. In

which case, I both understand and remain most unfailingly, your humble servant and admirer.
    Sincerely,
    Silas Grange

Placing the letter in an envelope, he poured wax and sealed it. Having done so, he leaned back in his chair and stared at the ceiling. There was more light in the higher part of the room, a golden effulgence that still filled the spaces softly. Through the window he could see the complacent glow of light on the water of the Solent.

Perhaps a quarter of an hour later, in the calm of the evening, in the last remaining visibility, Grange walked up to Mrs. Quill's house. There was no sign of light at the windows, yet neither were the curtains drawn. He raised the door knocker. No one answered it. He hovered for several seconds, then slipped the letter under the door.

As he was about to leave, it seemed to him that he heard, unmistakably, the sound of a woman's laughter. He walked round to the side of the house and listened again, but remained unable to detect the source of the sound. It was, he decided, merely a trick of imagination, perhaps a voice carried up from the foreshore below the house, reflected by water. He shrugged his shoulders and walked away.

11

*T*he following evening, a restlessness sent him out walking again. He persuaded himself it was a desire to observe the foreshore in such fine weather, but it was the animation of his imagination that sent him forth.

Salt had been the staple industry of Lymington since time immemorial. A good climate and a long, level shore had allowed the making of numerous flat pans which served as shallow reservoirs for salt water.

Walking toward Oxey, Grange gazed out over the marshes where the industry was predominant. Striding along the Woodside, the shoreline appeared covered in windmills, briskly turning in a southwesterly breeze as they pumped salt water into the pans. Winding inlets were filled at shallow tide with salt seawater. The entire land west of Lymington, from the harbor to Oxey and Pennington, and stretching beyond almost to Keyhaven, appeared to the wandering eye to consist of salt pans. As each pool evaporated, so more salt water was added, until the concentration built up into brine. The deeply salinated water was lifted to large cisterns from which it ran direct to be boiled in pans.

So ancient were the rites of saltmaking that it seemed almost to have developed its own ecology. In the concentrated brine pools there was only one organism that survived. It was the strangest little creature, the so-called Lymington shrimp, which was found nowhere else.

Apart from occasional windmills, the only other features that demanded attention on the level landscape of the marshes were the boiling houses themselves. They appeared like bricked and tiled barns. At first—with their roofs almost to the ground—they seemed like houses that have sunk into the earth's soft medium, and this gave their appearance a bizarre aspect. On closer inspection the large barn doors beneath the highly pitched roofs were mainly open, and even in the late evening workers could be seen inside stoking the fires or adding coal. Smoke and steam poured upward through the huge, squat chimneys. The roadways and paths in their lee were almost black with ashes. At any one time, looking out across the foreshores, the observer might see twenty in operation, the steam and smoke from each of their chimneys mixing into a gray cloud, so that at certain times Lymington's shores from Pylewell to Hurst appeared to have spawned a veritable devil's industry.

.   .   .

At Oxey, Grange halted briefly to gaze out over the marshes, then continued toward Pennington.

The light was always changing above water. The sea was a pale green, and the light itself seemed to take its hues of blue and turquoise off the water itself. Cloud shadows moved across its surface. At Pennington, he stood and stared out to sea. A brisk southwesterly was blowing through the Solent, bringing puffs of low cloud. Off Hurst Castle, in the narrows, the sea was flecked with white horses. Several sails were beating up from Southampton.

He breathed deeply the moisture-laden air, and glanced at the several solitary sails that plied the Solent. Off Lymington River, a two-masted merchant brig had anchored and was lying bow to wind while its crew, mere ants on the foredeck, unloaded barrels from the main hold into a large rowing boat to be transported ashore. Tackles and lead blocks had been fitted to the main yardarm of the merchantman, which was being used as a derrick.

A tall, flying sail emerged from behind Hurst Castle, a high single mast with two jibs, though the vessel beneath it seemed relatively small. As it swung east, he observed that it was sailing on a fast reach with full canvas, the boom laid out flat over the side. The vessel's straight stem and fast lines indicated that she was the *Antelope*, a Revenue cutter, ninety-seven tons and ten guns. Her big fore-and-aft rig was designed to tack to windward against any escaping merchantman or smuggler. Strictly speaking, she was on station between the Needles and Swanage, but in pursuit of his duty her commander, John Case, interpreted his brief widely.

Grange watched the vessel adjust her heading once again, the quick flutter of a jib as the sails were trimmed to a new course. Like a greyhound, she seemed to be heading directly toward Yarmouth, perhaps to pick up rations or mail. The incoming tide only served to accentuate her speed. She was almost flying. He could see her bow strike a swell, and a sheet of water rise higher than her topsides. But though she now seemed fixed on her course, and settled, without warning she swung upward into wind, weathered round with extraordinary swiftness, and bore off toward the main shore. The wind, which had fallen from her sails as she swung, now filled them again suddenly. Under this fresh power, she heeled to her gunwales and her big rig seemed to catapult her forward.

With a thrill of intuition, Grange sensed the fixity of her intention. It would seem that she was interested in the merchantman. A gust struck, she heeled more, the crew eased the great mainsail to keep her level and driving. In hardly a few minutes she seemed to have crossed to the anchored ship. Grange watched, scarcely breathing, as *Antelope*'s prow was aimed directly at the merchantman's midship. Now her speed and the tide appeared to be pulling her toward a certain collision.

In his own telescoped vision she seemed to have already collided, and he fully expected to see her bowsprit crumble and her mast fall. But at the last moment *Antelope* broke away downwind, then swung upwind under the merchantman's stern, all her sails flapping and thundering. At her bow stood a seaman with a grappling iron. Avoiding the stern of the merchantman with her bowsprit, the helmsman brought *Antelope*'s forward gunwale within a few feet of the aft topside. The grappling iron was thrown, with two strong jerks the holding was tested, then two men sprang the distance, hauling themselves aboard on the knotted rope. Grange saw a single spur of water fly from the boot of one of the men, like a wing of Mercury, and heard faintly on the breeze the sound of their impact on the merchantman's hull.

At the same moment as they embarked, *Antelope*'s commander used her momentum to swing away before her own masts become caught in the merchantman's overhanging yardarms, which now presented an extreme danger. The cutter's momentum gave her steerage way. The thunder of her flapping sails halted as they filled, and she picked up speed and separation, standing off with her ten small guns while her men checked that the business of the merchantman was lawful.

It was a beautifully timed maneuver, and tears rose involuntarily into Grange's eyes, tears of admiration and exaltation, for like virtually every one of his countrymen, he believed with some reason that no one mastered the seas like Britain. It might be frowned upon to weep in danger or distress, but the same was not true of joy. For an eighteenth-century English male could weep as happily as any Elizabethan, and put an Italian to shame.

Soon after knocking, Mrs. Thompson opened the door for him, as though she had been waiting for his return.

"My boots are muddy, Mrs. Thompson. There is a confounded amount of old water about on the roads."

"Let me put them in the kitchen, sir. I'll brush them when they are dry."

"Thank you." Grange sat down on the hall chair to remove his boots and handed them to her. Like two people exchanging gifts in some formal ceremony, Mrs. Thompson handed him his undershoes, which he slipped on.

As he walked up the stairs, Mrs. Thompson called after him.

"There's a letter for you, sir."

Grange paused, returned, and took the letter from her hand. "Thank you."

Mrs. Thompson, from her station at the stair's foot, studied him. Grange raised his eyes and stared into her own. Mrs. Thompson nodded briefly and departed. He split the envelope with his finger as he walked upstairs, withdrew the single sheet, then stood on the landing as he studied it.

Dear Dr. Grange,
   Thank you for your kind letter.
   I shall be away for two days, but wonder whether you could consider visiting me on Saturday, at four o' clock in the afternoon, if that is convenient.

*If it is, sir, I implore you that there is no need to reply, and I
will look forward to your company at the agreed time.*
Sincerely,
Celia Quill

Placing the letter back in the envelope, he ascended the stairs
in thoughtful mood and walked on quiet undershoes through
to his study.

12

Out of a desire to view at greater leisure the Walhampton foreshore, Grange decided to proceed beyond the turning that approached Barrows Lane by footpath, and instead continued along the edge of the riverside. When he had first arrived in Lymington, and was without many patients, he had walked along that shore so many times that he had almost memorized it foot by foot. It had drawn him because of its desolation.

Flooded each year several times by high spring tides, the area was unfit for human habitation. Yet precisely because of its privacy, the sense of kinship, almost ownership, of its lonely footpaths, the walk raised memories of his earlier days. The tang of seaweed and marsh mud was the same, and its salty pungency evoked sensations of a strange, desultory freshness. It was odd how the sense of smell had a way of re-creating passions whose cause had long since been forgotten. An echo of anguish, triumph, and gratification, and those rare concurrences of emotion that form like fresh colors.

There were several small, physical changes which oddly disturbed him. On a stretch of deserted marsh, perhaps half a dozen log cabins had been built to house sails and working gear of the fishing rowboats. Raised on stilts, they perhaps avoided the lesser of the spring tides, but dark tidemarks on their lower walls showed that they had not escaped unscathed. Several of the sad dwellings had been taken over by gypsies or forest migrants. The wasteground around them was strewn about with old barrels on which the hoops were already rotting. An elderly lurcher dog with pitifully thin ribs emerged slowly from beneath the piles of one dwelling and stood up to watch him, though it appeared to lack the energy to bark or make a commotion. According to some arbitrary whim, the light breeze changed direction and a stench of rotting and human excrement struck him. It was a scene of desolation where there had once been natural order. And yet he felt guilty too, not so much by the lack of charity shown to these poor vagrants, but by the willfulness of their condition. They could have thrown themselves upon the mercy of the parish and found accommodation and basic rations, yet they chose to live outside the Poor Laws because it was what they preferred. They aggrieved him not least because they offended his notion of charity.

Apart from the elderly dog, there was no sign of the inhabitants. They were either hiding inside or had gone forth to forage on the foreshore.

He approached Barrows Lane in thoughtful mood, and climbed the footpath toward Mrs. Quill's house. Once inside the gate, however, the garden exerted its magical effect of causing him to lose all other cares. Halting on the flagstones which led to the house, he paused briefly to consider the view he most loved, that over the gray Solent toward the white and gold cliffs opposite Hurst.

"It is a pleasure to see you again, sir."

"Thank you."

Mrs. Quill invited him to sit down, then stood facing him, a slight smile on her face.

"You look well. Your duties do you good. Though you seem thinner."

"I am always thin, madam. We most of us eat too much."

"You think we women should be sylphs, perhaps?"

"No, not women. I think women look better with a little weight. Women are naturally . . . rounder."

Grange coughed embarrassedly. Mrs. Quill smiled.

"Indeed." She turned toward the window, staring out. "You wish me to continue, sir?"

"When we last spoke, madam, of a perfect gentle knight, you startled me somewhat by your suggestion that I might play the role."

"And why was that?"

"Because, it seems to me, in this role there are no certain qualifications."

"That is so."

"I do not mean things spiritual, but physical. I am not fit for the part—being thin, somewhat frail, and with regard to my looks, madam, I am as far from handsome as I should think it possible . . ."

"Sir, you suffer a delusion. I find your ignorance affecting. Men are so obsessed by looks that they believe they are reflected by the other sex. It is not so. Women are sometimes carried by a pretty face in a man, but it is not the rule. It is something that is deeper that affects us, and what that is you have, sir, in sufficient quantity. As a woman, let me be your judge."

"Evidence of it there is precious little. I am a quiet bache-lor . . ."

"And much admired by the fairer sex, by all accounts. If I did not know you better, I would say you fish for compli-ments."

"No, no, madam. There is no evidence. Let us say we disagree. But I would raise a fresh and final point."

"What might that be?"

"Of women I am nervous, shy. Oh, I am used to being solitary. I was not brought up to touch, or exchange emotion. I do not complain, I am used to it. In my work a certain detachment is perhaps necessary. I merely say that in matters of the heart, I am cold, I feel this barrier . . ."

"Barriers are made to be crossed."

"My barrier is internal. And it is voluntary."

"You seek my help, perhaps, as I seek yours?"

"Madam . . ." Grange hesitated. "Your thoughts are too swift for me. I have never asked for help other than to be left alone . . ."

"Then for my part, sir, you give me reason to demonstrate my own intentions and commitment. Sacrifice thus leads to sacrifice. If I may do you a favor, then you may be more inclined to me and our proposed agreement."

"I do not fully understand."

Yet Mrs. Quill appeared to show no signs of impatience, except that certain doubts may perhaps have cautioned her, or at least determined her, to proceed more evenly. Perhaps she was adjusting, as he might be, to the rapid movement of her own thought. She allowed several moments to pass, so that when she spoke, she did so quietly and deliberately.

"If you should wish it, I would help you with this . . . barrier between your self and what you might be, sir."

"Now I perceive you, madam. You are a very general of your thoughts . . ."

"And you, I think, understand me."

"I say, rather, that I admire you."

"And . . . ?"

"If you will forgive my slowness, I will say further that you do me such an honor with your sacrifice that—I cannot but accept."

So at four in the afternoon, or shortly afterward, on a Saturday, Grange rose from his chair and stood facing Mrs. Quill. She took his hand and looked into his face.

"I believe in you I have my best accomplice. Let me guide you to your best endeavor."

Grange nodded merely, outwardly calm, though inside he felt speechless with pride and terror.

"Then to practicalities. My maid is away today, visiting relations. Since I was intending to attend a dinner engagement this evening, I had no need of my cook and she too has a holiday. Earlier this afternoon, however, I heard that my hostess unfortunately has taken with a chill, and therefore it would seem the evening is mine. The house is ours, sir, if you wish to take advantage of it. Or are you called away?"

"No, madam. Nothing calls me but some papers, and there is nothing pressing in that."

"Then should you not inform your own housekeeper you will be away for supper? If you return in an hour, sir, I will prepare to meet you."

Grange smiled. "I will return as you suggest."

13

*C*almly, like one of those horse-drawn barges that drift
forward, until the animal gives a further tug, Grange walked
down the garden path away from Mrs. Quill's house. He was
propelled by an inner momentum which, because it was so
gentle, did not wake him from his reverie. In reflective mood,
he turned through the gate, then as if on impulse glanced back
and observed what he believed was Mrs. Quill's figure move

gently from the window into the interior of the house. He breathed in deeply and walked on.

"Thank you, Mrs. Thompson. I return briefly. I shall be away this evening. No supper is required."

Ascending the staircase, he noticed that Mrs. Thompson appeared to hesitate at her familiar station at the stair's foot:

"If a patient calls, sir, an emergency, what shall I inform them?"

"Tell them to call Dr. Hargood."

Because he prided himself on being available to his patients at most hours, it did not surprise him that Mrs. Thompson appeared perplexed. Anxiety showed on her face like anger, pulling the muscles together, tightening the mouth.

"I see, sir," she said, though it would appear that she did not.

Reaching his study, Grange poured a jug of water into a basin and splashed his face several times. He dried his face with a cloth and glanced briefly at himself in a mirror, surprised as always at what he saw there, at the strange, detached animal that lived within its depths. Glancing down, he noticed there was a trace of grime on the backs of his wrists, and a line of perspiration from his shirt cuffs. Sinking deeper into time, he poured water over his hands and began to wash. He seemed to hover there, not thinking precisely but lost in thought, as though between two worlds. The ceremony caused his body to become still and his mind to drift. He rinsed the soap off his hands carefully. His physical being seemed detached, distant. As if overhearing a conversation, he listened to the clank of the jug being replaced.

Yet Mrs. Quill exhibited no surprise at seeing him when he appeared at her door, and she stood aside to let him in. He heard the door close firmly behind him, and fancied that she leaned back on it for the briefest moment, studying him with affection. In the hallway again they faced each other. Mrs. Quill smiled and put her hand through his arm.

"Come, sir."

Together they walked up the stairs, then amiably, arm in arm, along the corridor, and through an open door into a room with, at its furthest reaches, a large four-poster bed. Mrs. Quill closed the door, and again he had the impression, fleeting as it may be, that she leaned on it, staring at him as though attempting to see through him. He turned and caught her eye and smiled back, more hesitatingly.

"Well, sir," she said.

"Well," Grange replied.

Mrs. Quill started to unclasp the fastenings on her dress. Still somewhat dazed, he watched her for a few seconds, astounded at her quiet decisiveness. Glancing upward, she noticed his hesitation.

"Let me lead you."

She removed her dress with the calmness of a judgment; her stockings; then slid off her slip. He removed his jacket, shirt, boots. As he fumbled with the knee fastenings of his breeches, she walked naked by him, to the bed, and pulled the covers over her. He continued to remove his breeches.

"Come to bed, sir."

Naked finally, he joined her. Yet once beneath the sheets, for several minutes their bodies lay without movement, while the gray light seemed to move about them. In this, her calm province, she exhibited no sign of nervousness, but perhaps waited for his own fluttering heart to subside.

Lying beside him, she turned to face him, placing a hand on his shoulder, staring into his face.

"I repeat, sir, that you should let me lead."

He looked into her gray eyes, which in turn seemed to regard him with composure, absorbing his expression, amused within themselves. She kissed his face. He felt the calmness of her breath as she moved slowly to his neck and shoulder, and closed his eyes.

. . .

Afterward they lay side by side in bed, separate but amiable. It was darker, almost half-light. Of their two faces, Mrs. Quill's was the more composed. Half smiling, she seemed to gather her thoughts from the air about her. Grange's face was more thoughtful.

"You are a most attentive pupil," Mrs. Quill hardly whispered, so that this, breathed into the air above, was almost an observation to herself.

"Good teachers make attentive pupils, madam."

She pursed her lips, considered. "It is getting dark. Stay here. I shall light a candle."

Grange watched as she rose from the bed, confident in her nakedness, drew on her shift, and left the room.

For several minutes Grange's eyes idly traced the outline of the room. The small window was partly obscured from his view by the canopy of the bed, yet the light itself seemed obscure, lemon or amber in its coloring, and he sensed, rather than observed, the stillness of a sky darkening and about to rain. A short while later Mrs. Quill returned with a lit candle in a holder and placed it beside the bed. He glanced at her clothed figure as she sat down beside him, at the curves which suggested themselves beneath her shift, the calmness of her profile. She smiled down at him from her sitting position, leaning over him, and with her hand began slowly to pull down the sheet covering him.

"Come, sir, we must continue our researches. One lesson follows another."

Though still in her shift, she raised a knee and placed herself astride him, staring down into his face, and when she had finished gazing, drew off her shift, so that the white cloth seemed to rise like a flame, exposing breast and belly. Her eyes never left his face, she did not once falter in her gaze, but after a while leaned forward slowly, bringing her lips to his.

. . .

It was Mrs. Thompson who sat in her small parlor fretfully awake. A clock ticked loudly. A thunderstorm which seemed to have arisen over Pennington perturbated in the distance. She heard footsteps in the street outside, and several times raised her face from staring at the small fire in her room which she had lit to ward off the evening chill. Against her ample, starched bosom she polished an apple as rosy as her heated cheeks. A few seconds later, there was the spit and crack of thunder. After thunder the silence seemed deeper. In its lee Mrs. Thompson repeated to herself a question that seemed to have taken hold in her mind:

"Do women's souls sing?"

She shook her head at the absurdity and, as if through anger or in private consolation, bit into the apple greedily.

Like passengers on a liner that is moving them to a different destination, Mrs. Quill and Grange lay satiated on the bed, their bodies white in the candlelight. The sheets had been drawn off, for the heavy air was humid. Grange was sleeping peacefully. Mrs. Quill lay awake, staring at the ceiling with her fine eyes, a half smile on her lips.

Yet when he woke he would not stay the night there, believing, not without reason, that his absence overnight would raise the fury of Mrs. Thompson's suspicion.

At half past eleven Mrs. Thompson was roused from her fretful sleep by strong knocking at the front door. In her befuddled state, the first aspect of which she became aware was the rain, so strong it was like a physical pressure on the roof, a constant low hiss or hum as she made her way to the front hall. Runnels could be heard in the street. She raised the spyhole, then swung the door open. In what seemed to her an explosion of heavy rain, Dr. Grange entered like a sea creature, carrying water on him in white patches, shedding them as he swung the heavy door closed. His muddy boots made a puddle on the floor. She stood back to look at him.

"Why, sir," Mrs. Thompson exclaimed, "you're soaked!"

"I am back, Mrs. Thompson." Grange removed the great-coat. "A little wet, I grant."

Some aspect of him made her afraid. Mrs. Thompson observed that he was exultant, his face shining. At this time of night he seemed to her like a seal or merman, white with salt. At arm's length she reached out to hold the huge, wet great-coat that Mrs. Quill had lent him so that he might travel home.

"And who does this belong to, sir?"

"A friend. Were there any emergencies?"

"No, sir."

He nodded and began to ascend the stairs, with that same strange momentum and resolved force, and it occurred to her at the same time that the upper stairwell and landing were both unlit, that he seemed prepared to penetrate the obscurity without benefit of light. She held her own flame high so that some small radiance would be shed on the stairs, and as he traveled upward into darkness, she called:

"If you leave your clothes outside your room, sir, I'll wash and dry them."

"On the landing," Grange said, turning for her benefit, though she could hardly see him now. "I will leave them on the landing."

Mrs. Thompson peered up the stairwell at his disappearing form, listening as his heavy boots traversed the landing, observing the creak and then the peremptory, unconditional slam of his bedroom door. He was possessed of a vivacity that seemed like exaltation, or like anger. She was still standing there, gathering her thoughts, when the door opened and her master's clothes, heavy with water, were swung hard over the banister like a discarded pelt. The door slammed again.

Only in the weighted silence that followed, under the weight of her surprise and agitation, did she think to whisper under her breath, "Do men's souls sing, I ask myself?"

14

*Y*et the following morning, on Sunday, Grange appeared
listless, cast into his own thoughts, and ate his breakfast without enthusiasm.

When Mrs. Thompson entered with a plate of ham, placing
it on the table before him with her usual firmness, he seemed
so much party to his own thoughts that she suspected he was
not aware of her presence at all. She was almost departed by

the time he had asked a question, which nevertheless caused her to pause.

"Would you like me to tell you where I was last night, Mrs. Thompson?"

Mrs. Thompson, sensing a mode of irony, feigned indifference.

"No, sir."

Grange nodded and merely said, "Then I will not."

Though he showed little enthusiasm, he ate several slices of ham mechanically, and washed them down with tea. Several minutes later, when she entered to clear the plates, she found that Grange was standing by the window and staring out across the road toward the Lymington rivermouth. Passing the door on some errand in the kitchen, Mrs. Thompson noticed him again. His position had not changed. She took care to pass the doorway several times in the interval that followed. After a few moments she noticed that he shrugged, sighed slightly, and without glancing in her direction went upstairs to his study.

On Sunday mornings, since he did not visit church on principle, owing to his radical beliefs, he had formed the habit of retreating to his study in the hours that would otherwise be spent in piety—that is to say, praying to a God whose existence he devoutly questioned, singing hymns whose provenance offended him, or listening to some Tory vicar expostulating on the sins of the world. Instead, he preserved those times for reading a book of his own choice.

Mrs. Thompson, on the other hand, attended church, though she went not to St. Thomas, but to the Reformed Church which had not long since been constructed. He might prefer the stimulus of new thought, but she preferred the known. Even though her church was new, what she loved was the familiar, the well tried and tested. There was no pleasure for her in change. He heard her pause in the hallway, open the door, and a few seconds later observed her through his study window, which overlooked the High Street. Her shawled figure made its way across the pavement and disappeared from the angle of his vision.

From his position at the desk, he could hear occasionally the raised voices of passers-by, though it was a quiet time and generally speaking they did not disturb him.

His text was Hume, his choice of subject the origins of pride and humility.

But though pride and humility have the qualities of our mind and body, that is self, for their natural and more immediate causes, we find by experience, that there are many other objects, which produce these affections, and that the primary is, in some measure, obscured, and lost by the multiplicity of foreign and extrinsic. We found a vanity upon houses, gardens, equipages, as well as upon personal merit and accomplishments; and tho' these external advantages be in themselves widely distant from thought or a person, yet they considerably influence even a passion, which is directed to that as its ultimate object. This happens when external objects acquire any particular relation to ourselves, and are associated or connected with us. A beautiful fish in the ocean, an animal in a desert, and indeed any thing that neither belongs, nor is related to us, has no manner of influence on our vanity, whatever extraordinary qualities it may be endowed with, and whatever degree of surprise and admiration it may naturally occasion. It must be some way associated with us in order to touch our pride. Its idea must hang in a manner, upon that of ourselves; and the transition from the one to the other must be easy and natural.

For perhaps the course of nearly two hours he read, absorbed and delighted, working backward and forward through the sentences so that he could gather further their meaning, though certain passages continued to elude him. Such was his concentration, his two hours were no sooner begun than there was Mrs. Thompson's hand at the door, she having let herself in the side entrance, enquiring whether he would like a tea.

. . .

After he had finished his tea the restlessness took hold of him again, and he felt an inner compulsion to go out and take the air. It was his experience that the action of brisk perambulation drove morbid thoughts from the mind.

Besides which, he enjoyed walking on Sunday, amid evidence of other businesses and operations that flouted the rules of the Sabbath. Summer being their crucial season for evaporating water, many of the salt pans continued to function throughout the seventh day in the midsummer months, and on this day Grange deliberately set out to walk past them on his way to Pennington.

Several times while out walking on previous Sundays, Grange had met Briggs, the local Salt Officer, skulking along the roads. Once he discovered Briggs lying on the bank of a dry ditch, peering through a telescope at certain operations that were taking place out on the Woodside marshes.

"Indeed," Grange commented as he walked past, hoping to evoke in Briggs some sign of embarrassment at his spying activities, but Briggs refused to budge or acknowledge him. There was a certain sympathy in Grange for the plight of the Salt Officer. It was a miserable work, underpaid at £40 a year. Briggs's duties included that of being present at the sale and removal of salt, supervising the weighing, and recording the amounts of the many salterns in the neighborhood. To prevent corruption in the form of collusion with the owners of the Salterns, it was deliberate policy that Salt Officers were circulated every four years. For this reason a Salt Officer could never settle fully into a community. He was an outsider, an official who hovered on the periphery like a vagrant or criminal. For such Grange always felt a sense of fellowship.

Hargood too was tolerant of Salt Officers, except for a certain Gabriel Symes, headquartered at Buckler's Hard, whose habit it had been to creep by the foreshore at Pylewell in order to observe the Lymington Salterns on the other side of the river. Grange had heard the story before, and hoped he might hear it again. For the incident or opportunity occurred, as it happened, also on a Sunday, when Hargood usually gave brief sanctuary to the birds and beasts of his extensive lands from his virile feats of arms.

It seemed that Symes took advantage of the church attendance, and the evident lack of people in the fields and footpaths, to carry out his more secretive surveillance. There was a stretch of open foreshore in front of Hargood's house, and set back a little from the marsh, on firmer ground, a ragged line of shrubs and sturdy holly bushes that afforded his grounds a little privacy from those who worked upon or traversed the foreshore. Having taken horse from his cottage in Norley Wood, Symes was in the habit of taking a footpath that ran alongside Hargood's property in order to reach the foreshore.

Hargood, having defined his target, bided his time until he observed Symes, in the interests of taking up a camouflaged position, back a few yards up the shingle into Hargood's land. There Symes took up residence amongst several of the holly bushes that lined the seaward edge of Hargood's property. It was to Hargood's advantage that Symes, his attention concentrated on the scene ahead of him, did not focus much on the landward side. Perhaps he calculated that the physician too would be seated amongst other pious worshippers at the Boldre church.

Hargood, as it happened, had attended early Communion that morning, and not being one to take too much of a good thing, at least in spiritual matters, had desisted from Matins. So, in his turn, having made his peace with his God, and observing Symes's maneuvers on the edge of his land, he made advantage of the opportunity to take hold of a fowling piece which he habitually kept loaded in the pantry, filled with buckshot. With some brief words of forgiveness to his Maker for taking arms, in however good a cause, he crept down the slope, keeping to the copses and shrubs so that he closed, unobserved, to within seventy yards of the target. Symes faced away, his telescope extended, showing his broad aft sections. Hargood, presented with such a target, aimed and let fire, causing Symes, in Hargood's own words, "to rise into the air like a startled partridge," snap his telescope shut, and "to flee along the foreshore, uttering loud whoops of rage."

It was perhaps typical of Symes's effrontery that it was to Hargood that he came, the Monday following, to request that the doctor remove three pellets from his rear, and while Hargood examined him, Symes was heard to mutter darkly that but for the thickness of his breeches and his coat, there would have been a dozen or so more woundings. It was perhaps also typical of Englishmen that neither should mention directly the cause of the injury, or allude to the events that led to it. Besides which, there operated between them a delicate, symmetrical and mutual blackmail whereby, if Symes had brought prosecution for assault with a dangerous weapon, so Hargood would have cited trespass and spying on the Sabbath, which, given the status of Salt Officers, would not have been well received by any local magistrate, who might even have approved of the brisk action taken.

As it was, Hargood removed the pellets with tweezers, applied concentrated vinegar as astringent, and dressed the wounds. But out of a certain delicacy and good taste, having displayed his disapproval in such measured terms already, he did not charge Symes for the service.

In good heart after his walk, Grange returned. Mrs. Thompson let him in. "There's a letter for you, sir."

"Oh?"

"A young lady brought it."

Mrs. Thompson allowed her eyes to move downward to the letter in her hand, then she raised her eyes toward his, and he observed in their interior an enquiry concerning him, an enquiry which he was unable to answer. He took the letter, and would have thanked her, but was concerned by her candid expression of surveillance. Lost for a few seconds, he nodded to her and was about to start up the stairs when, just as suddenly, with a brisk movement of her dress and her voluminous hips, she turned and was gone.

In the sanctuary of his study he opened it with some deliberation.

> *Dear Dr. Grange,*
>
> *I asked my youngest daughter, Jane, who visits me today, to deliver this letter to you.*
>
> *So much I have to thank you for, kind sir, I do not know where to start. I know in you I have found my perfect collaborator.*
>
> *My daughter is here for a few days only, and will leave at the end of the week. I wondered if you would care to join us for supper. My cook is away, so such nourishment as we may offer would be light. If you would forgive us our poor fare, we would be most pleased to see you at six tomorrow evening.*
>
> *The likelihood is that you are busy with your papers. I do not wish to burden you with a reply, or the necessity of walking to this house merely to deliver your answer. Suffice it that we will be eating at seven, sir, and as is becoming increasingly my practice, if we may see you, we will see you.*
>
> *I remain gratefully yours,*
> *Celia Quill*

So it was that Grange stood up, restless, thinking. Mrs. Thompson entered the room with a tray.

"You left your tea untouched, sir. I thought I'd bring you a second."

"Thank you, Mrs. Thompson."

She set down the tray, directed a surreptitious glance at the letter on his desk, observed him watching her, and departed. As she disappeared through the door, he called:

"Oh, Mrs. Thompson."

"Sir?"

"I shall be going out tomorrow evening. I have been invited to share a light supper."

"A light supper," Mrs. Thompson repeated, as though allowing the phrase time to air, to give forth its secret scents. "Thank you, sir."

15

*O*n the following day, appointments pressed too closely to allow Grange the luxury of walking. Traveling to Hargood's house, it was necessary to take his horse, which was stabled at an ostlery behind the Hope and Anchor, and to ride across Walhampton Bridge, paying the tollgate keeper one and a half pence for man and beast. Thereafter he proceeded along the foreshore, striking inland for almost two miles until he reached the driveway and Hargood's fine Palladian house. Tying the reins of his horse on a nearby railing, Grange opened the gate and knocked on the door. Hargood opened it himself, clad in dark breeches and heavy riding boots.

"Silas, my good fellow. Come in."

"Thank you."

"Go through to the sitting room. I will take off these boots."

Good host that he was, Hargood behaved as if this unexpected visit had been planned. After shaking hands warmly, he stood aside, sat down on the hall bench to draw off his boots, then followed Grange into the hall. The rooms inside that could be perceived from the hallway were filled with paintings, hunting trophies, large pieces of furniture. Hargood caught up with Grange in the inner hallway. Together, Hargood's hand on his shoulder, they walked through to the sitting room.

"You've been riding?" Grange asked.

"Never miss a morning's gallop, if I can help it. Now, may I offer you a drink, dear fellow?"

"No, thank you."

Hargood released Grange's shoulder and stood before him, his right eyebrow raised.

"I came to ask a favor," Grange began.

"Drive at me, sir. I owe you enough myself."

"I may have a number of engagements which will take me away from my work. If there are emergencies, I wonder if I could adopt my usual practice of directing any patients in need of immediate attention to you?"

"Of course, of course. It's only fair." Hargood winked. "Except when I may be in London, of course."

"Thank you."

"Silas, you are a mystery to someone such as myself. Here you are, a successful practitioner, an eligible young man, and yet you're so damned withdrawn. You seem to have no fun. I sincerely hope that these engagements of yours are with a lady friend."

"With a friend who is a lady."

"Good, that's a start. You want some advice? Don't consort

with local women. It becomes public. Damn it, you should do what I do. Take a mistress in London, visit her at least once a two-month, stay a week, and come back exhausted and refreshed and all the better for it. Eh?"

"What you suggest is sensible . . ."

"Of course it is. It's good to get away from this place too. Staying here all the time would make me morbid. Between riding my horses here and my mare in London, I have the best of both worlds. And by the way, I thank you again for looking after my patients when I'm away." Hargood studied Grange benignly. "You're well?"

Grange nodded. "In good health."

"In body, I am sure. How do you keep so thin? That studious nature, perhaps. Do you eat? Or do you merely imbibe the refined vapors of books? I'll be damned." Hargood paused and stared. "You're not in love, are you? Dangerous thing, love. Bachelor's worst enemy. Only love or impotence can deflect a determined man from pleasure—and love's by far the worst. Well, answer me."

"Yes, I do eat, Hargood." Grange weighted his reply with the mere hint of a smile.

Hargood glanced at him, then laughed outright. "You always were a sly one, Silas. If you won't tell me about your lady friend—your friend who is a lady—is there anything else upon which I can give you the benefit of my vast experience?"

"You've already helped me enough, and I am grateful."

"And Silas, you are in good heart? You do not work too hard, I hope?"

"I am in good heart, and work as usual. I am afraid I cannot test your hospitality further, kind though you are. I have an appointment in half an hour."

Grange smiled at his host, but showed no sign of sitting down and was clearly determined to depart.

"Going already? Well, I'll see you out. Mrs. Thompson in good health?"

"In excellent health."

"Keeps you in line, I hope. She's too good for you, of course. Makes you complacent. There is one thing I wanted to say, while you're here." Hargood halted in the hallway so that Grange, swung like a weight on the pendulum of his host's concern, pivoted to face him. "My patient, Mrs. Celia Quill." Hargood paused. "You've been seeing her recently?"

"A social visit, sir."

"Silas, Silas, my boy, I know you well enough to know you aren't stealing my patients. No, my dear young fellow, that isn't my line of interest. I'm just saying, be careful. That's a strong-minded woman. Attractive, too."

"Be careful?"

"Careful," Hargood repeated. "*Cave*, Latin, beware."

"Beware of what?" Grange asked, aware that the silence collected uneasily around his question.

"Beware, I say, of strong-minded, handsome women."

"Who are also local?" Grange forced a brief smile. "These warnings have a certain circularity."

"Well, there you have it, sir," Hargood commented affably. "I know there's a part of you that's sensible."

Grange moved toward the door, Hargood accompanying him. At the door Grange turned to say his farewell, yet Hargood's face again was serious.

"Silas, you are a most studious man, and perhaps I could leave you with a certain thought. Sometimes, in life, we see great souls emerge from strange surrounds."

"Indeed."

"The son of a butcher becomes a cardinal. The tenth son of a poor rector becomes a great admiral. I know this seems strange, but imagine, my dear fellow, that one of these great and terrible souls appeared in petticoats, with the body and instincts of a woman. She would have no outlet. She must live with all the restrictions of her sex. What sort of woman would that be?"

"You are very philosophical, suddenly."

"I am not, I assure you, by disposition. I have merely asked you a question. I hope that you keep it in some recess of that scholarly mind."

"As you say."

Hargood patted Grange amiably on the shoulder and opened the door.

Grange shook his hand. "Good-day, Hargood."

"Good-day, Silas." Hargood paused, and then added one final, parting shot. "Silas, you're a calm and rational man. And with Mrs. Quill—I merely give my opinion—that makes you a lamb before a wolf."

"A lamb before a wolf," Grange repeated, and nodded, as if the concept presented some remote quandary, which could only be revealed by close study. He nodded again, saying only, "I do note what you say."

"And having noted, you will ignore it entirely. To hell with you, sir," Hargood said, and closed the door amiably on his younger associate. But it was noticeable, when he had lowered the crossbar and leaned against it, that Hargood's face took up an attitude of utmost seriousness. And he remained there in thought for the best part of a minute.

16

Seated at his desk, Grange leaned forward, his elbows on the table, so that he could study the book with greater intensity. He read to himself from David Hume's *A Treatise of Human Nature:*

> *'Tis now time to turn our view from the general consideration of sympathy, to its influence, on pride and humility, when these pas-*

sions arise from praise and blame, from reputation and infamy. We may observe, that no person is ever praised by another for any quality, which wou'd not, if real, produce of itself a pride in the person possest of it. The elogiums either turn upon his power, or riches, or family, or virtue; all of which are subjects of vanity, that we have already explained and accounted for. 'Tis certain, then, that if a person consider'd himself in the same light, in which he appears to his admirer, he wou'd first receive a separate pleasure, and afterwards a pride of self-satisfaction, according to the hypothesis above explain'd. Now nothing is more natural for us to embrace the opinions of others in this particular; both from sympathy, *which renders all their sentiments intimately present to us; and from* reasoning, *which makes us regard their judgment, as a kind of argument for what they affirm. These two principles of authority and sympathy influence almost all our opinions; but must have peculiar influence, when we judge of our own worth and character. Such judgments are always attended with passion; and nothing tends more to disturb our understanding, and precipitate us into any opinions, however unreasonable, than their connexion with passion; which diffuses itself over the imagination, and gives an additional force to any related idea. To which we may add, that being conscious of great partiality in our own favour, we are particularly pleased with anything, that confirms the good opinion we have of ourselves, and are easily shocked with whatever opposes it.*

He continued to read until that point, which he always reached with Hume, when his mind swam with thoughts and felicities, and he put the book aside so that, out of a cloud of imaginings, he could select and consider a few points that were strange to him, that he had not noticed before. As he closed the volume, the pages fell open at a particular place, and he noticed briefly the phrase

. . . the senses alone are not implicitly to be depended upon, but that we must correct their evidence by reason, and by considerations, derived from the nature of the medium. . . .

. . .

On the ground floor, Mrs. Thompson paused from sewing one of Grange's shirts, and directed her attention to the creak of the floorboards as he moved across the study. There was a special means, it seemed to her, by which particular states of mind imparted different qualities and intensities to the sound. During working mornings, for example, when he prepared for surgery, his perambulations were brisk, and the sounds that came from them emphatic, like his imagined state of mind. In the grip of concentrated thought, however, the footsteps seemed to drift, and the sounds themselves came from no particular area, but merely appeared briefly on one side of the room and then another. It seemed to her that in some strange manner the thoughts themselves made such noises through the thinking medium of his body. Now, pausing from the lively work of the needle, she heard the movement of a chair in the study, followed by silence. Poised, she remained in that position for several seconds; then, perhaps reassured that he had settled, she returned to her sewing.

Grange, having pondered at the window, returned to the desk and continued to read. He glanced up at the clock, then back at the surface of the book.

> *Reason, being cool and disengaged, is not motive to action, and directs only the impulse received from appetite or inclination, by showing us the means of attaining happiness or avoiding misery. . . .*

After some further time spent in reading, during which he was unaware of his external circumstances, as if sunk into the pages themselves, he paused to consider the results of what he had been studying. Under the impetus of thought, the clock's beating appeared to grow louder, then inexplicably softer. He put the book gently aside, sighed, rose, stretched.

. . .

Mrs. Thompson halted her sewing again to listen to Grange pacing his room. Then she heard him descending the staircase. She set down her sewing, placed the thimble on the small sewing tray she kept beside her, heaved herself to her feet, picked up the heavy, black garment drying by the fire, and went out to the hall to meet him.

"Your cloak, sir."

"Thank you, Mrs. Thompson."

Mrs. Thompson opened the door and closed it behind Grange. She was tempted to go to the window in the front parlor, to view his disappearing back, but she knew without resorting to observation which direction he would take. He was walking down the High Street, toward the river bridge, and thereafter would turn along the foreshore to Walhampton.

Mrs. Quill stood back from the doorway. "You have not suffered a chill, I hope?"

She took his cloak. Relieved of the garment, he turned to face her, imbibing a deep breath, and while she considered him with her calm gray eyes, he nevertheless felt impelled to press ahead at the earliest to inform her of his thoughts.

"Madam, I have thought long and hard about our discussion, and though I am flattered by your most kind attention and good expectations of me, yet . . ."

Before he was able to finish his sentence, Mrs. Quill put her finger to her lips and he, distracted, watched their soft expression in the implied negation. Her silence was an announcement, a felicity he did not appreciate until, appearing round the corner there emerged into his sight a slender figure. He was drawn suddenly from the expression on Mrs. Quill's lips to this new phenomenon. Emerging from the sitting room, the delicate creature halted, as surprised by him as he was by her. In her natural liveliness of expression, he noticed a resemblance to his hostess, though in her reticence there was something hidden. Though he did not normally notice clothes, it was the very simplicity of her garments that he remembered— a single long dress of red silk, tucked on the arms, and the rest freely hung, floating, so that, recognizing one another's presence, she did not so much move but drifted toward him.

"My daughter Jane," Mrs. Quill said. "Jane, this is Dr. Grange."

As she moved toward him, Grange was subject to a compendium of effects, in which the grace of her walk, the slenderness of her neck, the simple beauty of her dress, formed merely part of his impression.

She halted in front of him: "I am honored to meet you, sir."

Grange kissed her proffered hand.

"I am pleased to meet you."

"Shall we go through to the dining room?" Mrs. Quill asked, turning and leading the way.

The dining table was laid out for three. Mrs. Quill addressed Grange directly.

"Please do us the honor, sir, to sit at the head of the table."

The two women sat down, one on either side of him.

Mrs. Quill said, "We have some cold meats—leftovers, I fear. I'll fetch the soup."

She left the table.

"My mother speaks well of you, sir."

"Please call me Silas. Your mother insists on calling me, most formally, sir, even though we are sufficiently acquainted"—he paused briefly, at a loss, attempting to hide his embarrassment—"to be on Christian name terms."

"Mother is formal."

Recovering, Grange asked, "Where did you travel from today?"

"From Winchester."

"You live there?"

"My husband lives there. I will return in a few days time."

Mrs. Quill returned with the soup tureen. She placed it on the table, sat down, and leaning forward, ladled out a plate for Grange; then she filled plates for her daughter and herself.

"Jane," Mrs. Quill said, "I hope you have not been too much advanced with Dr. Grange."

"Your daughter is most kind, madam. I would beg that you put aside formality and call me Silas."

"Since you ask me, I will do so without hesitation."

They began the meal. Mrs. Quill, as she raised a spoonful of soup, observed the briefest glance that Grange directed at her daughter and smiled directly at him, as though in approval, which caused him again to consider her attitude. There was a stutter of thunder outside. Then it began to rain.

"What weather. Silas, I feel so guilty at your last departure in the middle of a thunderstorm, I would most certainly ask that you stay the night, and so proceed dry tomorrow morning."

"I thank you, madam. But I have patients whom I must see tomorrow."

"As indeed you shall, rested from a good night's sleep in our spare bedroom." She smiled at him. Under siege from her good intentions, Grange hesitated, and she said, turning away, "So it is decided, then."

"You are most kind . . ."

"Good. When we are finished dinner, Jane will make a bed for you."

"Thank you."

Jane smiled. In the reprieve between thunder Grange asked: "And how do you find our small town?"

"Oh, I like it much," Jane replied. "The air is fresh."

"There are those," Grange said, "who will tell you that our New Forest air is like a sleeping draft on the senses, that it encourages a sleep from which we do not wake."

"You seem awake to me."

"In our dreams," Grange said, "all seem awake."

Mrs. Quill, for her part, calmly sipped her soup, content to listen as the other two conversed.

At a brief nod from her mother, Jane stood up and cleared the plates. Grange watched her surreptitiously. She passed close by to take his plate. As she did so he raised his eyes and looked full into the gray eyes of Mrs. Quill, who regarded him again expressionlessly, though apparently without any hostility or disapproval at his awareness of her daughter's presence. Outside, the rain stopped.

Grange said, "The weather has relented."

Mrs. Quill smiled.

"Only to start again, I am sure."

Grange nodded.

"You are right, I do believe."

Silence after rain was like the calm after music. The last notes lingered in the atmosphere, and the silence itself was heavy with their memory, as though framed by absent sound. Jane returned with fresh plates and set them down. She left and returned again with a large platter bearing a cold leg of lamb and placed it in front of Grange, before sitting down herself.

Mrs. Quill asked, "Will you carve, Silas?"

"Why, certainly."

In the charged silence Grange began to slice the meat. The two women watched him without speaking. He placed slices on each of the plates, passing one to each.

"You carve well, sir," Mrs. Quill commented.

"For one who lacks practice."

"Then you should practice more often," Mrs. Quill held calm eyes to his, "and on more lambs."

When he had finished carving, Mrs. Quill raised her glass for a toast.

"To practice," Grange said.

They toasted and drank.

In the scullery, Mrs. Thompson raised a small cloud of steam from the shirt as she applied the iron in brisk stabs. For some time now, the small skylight above her had rattled with water like a drum, and silver runnels had streamed across its surface. As she plied the iron, the flame from the candle spread over the side wall the extensive shadow of her bust. The steady, insistent motion of her arm caused the cloth of her underdress to rub against skin. A flush from her exertions covered her face. Pausing to turn the shirt over, she noticed the quietness as the rain ceased. Glancing upward, she turned over a garment, and with a brief sigh continued.

. . .

The meal ended, Mrs. Quill and her daughter rose and removed the plates, leaving Grange on his own for several minutes, as though out of respect for the privacy of his own
thoughts.

When they returned, Mrs. Quill said, "Jane, it is time you
prepared a bed for Silas."

Jane smiled and left.

"You should have an early night, Silas, if you have engagements tomorrow."

She placed a calm hand on his.

"Madam," Grange said, "I thank you for your hospitality."

17

*M*rs. Thompson settled by the fire and began, by stages, to nod off. There was thunder in the background and, complaining to herself, she rose to shut the window. Then she eased back in the chair, arranging the cushion so that it supported the small of her back. She had intended merely to settle until Dr. Grange returned that night. Instead, she gradually entered that half-sleeping, half-dreaming condition in which time seems suspended. In some part of her she was aware of the movement of natural forces, of distant thunder and renewed rain. She awoke at half past eleven, though not completely, enough only to observe, as if from a distance, the time of the clock, and to return to her dreaming.

Some time later she woke again, notifying herself merely that it was past one and there had been no knock at the door. It occurred to her then that he would not be returning that evening. Guessing that the weather had caused his hostess to suggest that he stay the night, the choice lay before her of returning to her bed or continuing to inhabit her present restful state in the chair. She was settled, comfortable and drowsy, and she decided that she would not make up her mind for a few minutes, persuading herself that he might still return that night. After that, her mind being less wakeful and agitated lest he return, she entered into a deeper sleep, which doused all further concern, and she did not rouse herself until the clock showed half past five and early dawn was already beginning to lighten the room.

The atmosphere was not so close, much rain having fallen. A chill in the air was a spur to rise finally, to wash her face with cool water, and then to change her undergarment. Drowsy still, the procedures were slow, and by the time she was finished her ablutions it was past six, and the young light was already strong. Now dressed again, and feeling slightly refreshed, she put a kettle on the stove, piled further logs into it, and while it heated she went to the stairs and checked that he had not returned by walking up several steps in order to observe whether his bedroom door was closed. But it was open, proof to her that he remained out, and she turned back to the kitchen.

He returned shortly after half past eight, looking refreshed and strangely cheerful. A thin sun was already out.

"My hostess persuaded me the weather was too inclement to make the return journey by foot last night, and invited me to stay overnight."

"Sir."

"I hope you were not too much inconvenienced?"

"No, sir, not inconvenienced. Would you like breakfast?"

"No, thank you. I ate sufficient before I left."

She was standing aside in the hall, to allow him to pass, and he was framed against the light of the still opened door, against which she observed the stubble of a day's growth of beard on his face. She tried to make out what it was that differed materially from the same one who had departed yesterday evening, but gave up her thoughts as he sat down and put aside his boots, before ascending the staircase in his stockinged feet.

Jane was like a prism. All day Grange thought of her as he moved about the town; not directly, but somewhere in his mind she took hold as a permanent presence. Rays of light moved outward from her. By means of the same, strange alchemy his thoughts were overlaid by the presence of Mrs. Quill herself.

Smells assaulted him on the High Street, dour odors as heavy as bodies. Down the alley the warm scent of bread rose toward him from Edwards's bakery. Hay and cut grass, the reassurance of horse and cow manure. A sharper tang of coal emanated from the blacksmith's forge. The town itself was like a body. It had its scents and its armpits. The small tannery beside the river released its presence over the buildings, a sudden stench from the dyers' yards. Sometimes Grange treated one of the men who worked there, and who had imbibed the organic odor into his pores. Mrs. Thompson, in order that the smell should not linger for days, opened windows and allowed cold air to circulate even into the kitchen.

Yet who was he to comment, or to criticize, moving like an errant ghost about his practice? As often as not, the prevailing southwesterlies drew the smoke from the salt pans over Lymington, depositing the ashes of coals on the brickwork. The sweet smell of brine overlaid on the town the further presence of the sea itself. They were like a subcutaneous layer, memory laid down like fat.

And at night, when the great braziers that burned outside the Town Hall had been doused, and the street was illumined only by soft light from the moon or stars, he drove upward, swinging his boots on the cobblestones, hearing their echoes in the irregular corners of houses, past pale lighted windows, the surface of the Solent white between the buildings on the southern side of the street. A horse neighed in the stables of the Ship Inn. There were French refugees in the town—bitter, impoverished gentlefolk who had landed here from France and whose circumstances would not permit them to move to London, where they might better petition for their rights and families. Some had been formed into a regiment, but their training was limited to little more than an occasional march or cutlass drill. A commotion in the Bugle was more often Frenchman fighting Frenchman. It began as a rumble, a movement and thudding, and then issued out like bad air into the street, bulky bodies and growling dogs or screaming women, an explosion of imprecations, sometimes cudgels and ringing swords.

They had their own physician, a small, mild Breton called LaPère. But despite the arguments, there were surprisingly few wounds. LaPère stitched occasional deep cuts, using a method that left a pattern of elegant cross-grains at the lip of the wound, like an African ritual tattoo. He was much prized by the rougher elements at upper Pennington, who brandished his surgical scars like rare medals. At the Nag's Head it was quieter; steam from the kitchen billowed out, its smell of gobbets of mutton and cabbage. There were fewer fights but more lethalities. It seemed to Grange that once every several years, a body was carried out under blackened canvas and a morose, silent Englishman was arrested, tried at Winchester for murder, and efficaciously hanged.

At night in his bed he heard animals, prowling dog, the droll lowing of a cow, beyond Walhampton the sharp scream of a vixen carrying clear across the river. Turning on his bed, he sometimes breathed out a name, like an imprecation, and when the echo of it lingered he wondered what it was that he had said. Like something sensed in darkness, he observed its presence, even though it fell outside the scope of light.

18

Staring fixedly at the sea the following morning, Grange did not hear footsteps behind him.

In the New Forest, it seemed to him, the air flew by like clouds. Water lapped the foreshore. Standing on the Walhampton shore, looking across the estuary, he was entranced by this physical vision. It seemed to him entire of itself, with trees and flowers, ocean and sky, stars and stones, animals and insects.

Yet it also occurred to him that there was, amid the poverty, a recklessness amongst the people. On the north wall of the chapel at Boldre was a wall tablet for a recent vicar, the Reverend William Gilpin, who, taking up his post in 1777, was astounded by the lawlessness of parishioners: "exposed to every pillage and robbery, from their proximity to the deer, the game, and the fuel of the New Forest, the lower class of parishioners being little better than a gang of gypsies."

A voice behind him said, "The sea is feminine and merciless, sir. She is violent in her niceties."

Grange spun around, and observed at a short remove his fellow physician, regarding him somnolently.

"Hargood."

"My dear fellow. I see you gazing forth, and I wonder to myself what it is that you consider so vehemently."

"It is idleness, I am afraid."

Hargood drew alongside, and looked out over the waters with him. The estuaries seemed to draw illumination. Gulls flew above the reflected light. Side by side they were silent for a few moments.

"I have still a full side of beef, hanging in my cold room. I fear if I do not finish it, it will go rotten."

"You invite me again? You are most charitable."

Against the light, a column of gulls hovered over a tiny black fishing craft moored to the Jack-in-the-Basket perhaps half a mile distant.

"I am thinking of the meat, my dear Silas. From a view of practicality, the sooner the better. Are you prepared to join me?"

"I am always prepared to be jackal to your lion, Hargood."

Hargood was pleased to consider this image, and said, "Even so, for my part, I still perceive you as a wolf in sheep's clothing."

"You have yet further animal metaphors, sir?"

"No more than are necessary to illustrate a point, I do believe. Let us consider our plans. What night is earlier than tonight?"

"Tonight it is."

Hargood nodded, turned on his heel, and walked back to the horse that he had tethered at some distance to a gatepost. It occurred to Grange that Hargood had deliberately dismounted so that he could surprise him on foot. He smiled at the thought of his mentor taking such trouble to stalk him. At the same time it occurred to him that he should be grateful, for his own sake, that he was not a Salt Officer peering out upon his nefarious duties.

Inevitably, wine having been taken, the conversation drew round to Mrs. Quill, and her reason for settling in Lymington. Hargood wondered what took up her time.

"She is charitable," Grange replied, her champion now more than ever, and concerned to deflect attention from her by appearing to accede to his host's request for information.

"Charity is cold, sir. It heateth not. Passion too may be cold. Only love is hot."

"I do not admire Mrs. Quill for her passions, whatever they may be."

"For what, then?"

"She is calm in her soul. She knows her own mind."

"You believe that to be a good thing? In a woman, I mean."

"Yes."

"How so?" Hargood asked. He lifted another forkful of meat to his mouth.

"Because I believe, in their character, women are the better for maturity."

"Why?"

"You press me, Hargood, as usual."

"And why not?" Hargood asked. "It affords good exercise. I love to sniff at warm details and cold traces. Answer my question, I beg you."

"Because at a certain age they begin to reject all the errors which society will place on them."

"Which errors now, Silas? You intrigue me."

"For example," Grange said, "that they are inferior to men, that they must act a secondary role, that their best hope and fortune is to marry a man who may dominate them and teach them the niceties of their position. Was it not Milton who said, 'Man must be for God, and woman for the God in him'?"

"Indeed, and what an excellent precept it is," Hargood said approvingly. "But please continue."

"Women begin, as I say, with the corruption of men's expectations."

"And then they improve?"

"In the main."

"How?" Hargood insisted.

"By returning, I do believe, to a form of innocence."

"And what does this innocence consist of?"

"It consists of learning what is corrupt."

"And what is that?"

"Everything that they are taught by men."

"Proceed yourself, sir, to admonish me. I do like to listen to madmen and eccentrics. They entertain the mind delightfully. And afterward we may go home and laugh."

"Hargood, you do encourage me. I shall do my best to entertain you, then."

"Continue, my dear Silas. Continue. Let us hear some more nonsense. I am very avid of entertainment."

"I submit, then, that as time proceeds, so women learn the error of what they have been taught by men. They learn to think and choose for themselves. They become their own character."

"That is innocence? You tell me, in all honesty, that is innocence?" Hargood was poised, incredulous, in his jaw a hovering solemnity. Yet his eyes indicated he was about to laugh.

"Yes, I do believe so. But if innocence shocks you, Hargood, if it offends your notions of virginity, chastity, and maidenhood, then let us choose another word. Let us say it is a form of purity."

"Let me see now. Women begin in corruption and proceed, through experience, to a kind of purity."

"Precisely."

"Well, I have heard many things. But I do believe"—Hargood ate his food with gusto, considering from a favorable perspective the many eccentricities and imbecilities that he had witnessed or overheard—"I do believe that to be quite one of the most entertaining."

"You are exceptionally kind."

"You think women who have reached this age of purity, this age where they know their own minds, are attractive?"

"By virtue of their minds, yes."

Hargood studied him amiably, as he would a friendly citizen from another continent.

"For this reason," Grange continued. "When one deals with them, one deals with a woman, pure and simple, not some reflection of men's minds."

"Reflection of men's minds? That is a good one. Dear me, yes. Young women are reflections of men's minds. Mature women are pure by virtue of being themselves. I like that exceedingly. Have you any more thoughts on this line?"

"No more on this issue, I would say. However, I believe that I may have done my duty, and entertained you enough for the time being."

"Indeed you have," Hargood said, "indeed you have. Here, have a little more meat, sir, and then perhaps I may live in hope that you will have the strength to entertain me some more."

"That is very well," Hargood said a short while later, determined to return to the subject, though perhaps content to lead in a different direction. "But to a man such as yourself, who is so fond of the minds of women, why do you not put your theories into practice, and marry one? Instead, you fill your thoughts with Hume."

"You do not understand, I think, my particular liking for Hume."

"Indeed I do not."

"Hume is not my Bible. He is my Lucifer, my devil. All that I assume, he attacks and subverts."

"He begins to sound to me like a damn good fellow," Hargood said. "What precisely does he attack?"

"He attacks the provenance of Reason. He argues that Reason by itself is meaningless. Before Reason may act, there must be something prior . . ."

"Prior?"

"Something else which precedes it. In mathematics, we say, let X be this or that, and thus proceed to argument. But there is always a prior assumption."

"In mathematics, perhaps . . ."

"In humans, too, I do believe. The prior or given consists of our emotions. Hume argues that Reason serves emotion, nor could it do otherwise."

"Why not?"

"Because Reason cannot exist on its own."

"You believe him?"

"He is, as I say, a very devil to contradict."

"How strange you are. You call yourself a rationalist, and subscribe to the deity of Reason, yet you study the very one who attacks your assumption most forcibly."

"Reason does not proceed by confirmation, but by contradiction. We know nothing of our arguments until we have heard the opposite. That is, sir, where I disagree with religionists, who in the main are infuriated by any statement which is the opposite of what they themselves choose to believe. If I may draw a difference between myself and them, it is not simply a case of my believing something else, but the methods I use to ascertain the truth of what I believe."

"You are very lucid tonight. Yet I must admit that it sounds perverse to me."

"Is it truly perverse, that you test what you believe against its opposite?"

"Tell me, sir," Hargood observed slyly, shifting his ground like a fencer, the better to drive home a thrust, "might this not also be your attraction to Mrs. Quill?"

In the middle of transferring a thin slice to his mouth, Grange paused, suddenly arrested. "Mrs. Quill?"

"That she is the opposite of you in some way? That you hope she will test you?"

"Sir, you place things abstract into personal terms."

"It is my role as physician, after all," Hargood said with something approaching satisfaction, "to apply the abstract to a personal level."

"In what way might she be my opposite?"

Hargood ate for several moments. He waved his fork as if about to announce something, and continued.

"That you are a rationalist, and she may be . . . the opposite."

"I find her very rational, I assure you."

"You do, do you? Then let us suppose that you might be opposites in another respect. That your motivation might be for one thing, and she for another."

"Which are opposite?"

"Indeed," Hargood said.

"Give me an example."

"Let us say, for theory's sake, you understand, that one of you might have good motivations, the other evil."

"I do believe that what you say is unlikely."

"Explain, sir." Hargood waved his fork encouragingly, and Grange, pausing to put down his own fork, answered:

"I do not believe in evil as a motivation."

"Why not?" Hargood was interested.

"Because I have not met it. I have met some mischief, I think, and numerous bitter differences of opinion. And I have met many who were torn between one course and another, or who pursued their own interest against others. But the idea of evil as a dark force, as original sin, seems to me absurd."

"And therefore, by the same token, you do not believe in the devil?"

"Indeed not, sir."

"And why not?" Hargood probed the side of his mouth with his tongue, searching for stray fragments.

"Precisely because I cannot conceive of him as a complete being."

"Complete? He is complete to himself, surely. You should account for your own opinions on this matter, I do believe."

"If he is slothful, how may he be, at the same time, so active, and rigorous, in the prosecution of this sloth? To pursue his supposed course of universal corruption, he must spread the doctrine of evil with the single-mindedness and dedication of a saint. If he pursues falsehood, to give another example, then he will tie himself in knots, unless he has himself the clearest idea of the truth."

"What point do you make, sir?"

"For the effective pursuit of any vice, it requires something like a virtue to drive it. That is the point I make. A being who is constructed entirely of evil is not a functioning being."

"Come now," Hargood said. "He knows the difference between good and evil, that is the point. And he pursues the latter."

"That is even more unbelievable, if I may say so. He knows happiness, and pursues unhappiness; he knows pleasure, and pursues pain; he knows virtue, and pursues vice. He knows love, and pursues hate."

"Well now, and how do you explain the destruction in the world, the injustice, without his baneful influence?"

"I attempt to explain it in this way. First, there are many ways of pursuing the good. And second, for every different notion of the good, there is a potential conflict with another."

"This is sufficient to explain the surfeit of evil?"

"The evil that I perceive arises out of conflicting goods. It seems to me self-evident that terrible destruction can result from precisely those who pursue differing or opposite notions of the good. If this is so, I do not need an additional theory of evil to explain the destruction I perceive in the world."

"Why not?"

"Because what I have posited is a simpler explanation. It is a matter of supplying Occam's razor."

"And how do you explain the robber, the brigand, the thief?" Hargood pressed his case.

"What should I explain in them?"

"The incidence of evil, the motivation that drives the malefactor."

"Each example you have given me seems an instance of a man pursuing his own interest against that of others. It is a sin, I believe, to place oneself above others, but it is one of which I myself am often guilty."

"You think, then, the robber is no different from you?"

"No different from me in motivation. I do not disagree with his aim, but with his method. It seems to me he is pursuing his own interest by harming others. You and I pursue our own interest, I would suggest, by attempting to help others, however unsuccessful we may be on occasion."

"The murderer, then? Pursuing the same aims, though with a different method?"

"The murderer is very rare, sir. I have not yet met one. And in trying to explain him, I can only describe that which I know. I know enough that people's senses may be disturbed, temporarily or permanently. I know enough of my own that I may be disturbed, I hope only temporarily. I have no direct knowledge of intrinsic evil, but I have one of disturbance. Therefore I apply what I know rather than what I do not know."

"Very commendable. And, in the meantime, Satan slips by unobserved."

"Does he?" Grange was determined not to let Hargood slip by unobserved. "In childhood we required our fears in human form. In raising the subject of the devil, is he not that fear of which you speak?"

"An embodiment of our fears, you mean?"

"Yes, or similar."

"You do not fear Satan?"

"No, in honesty I do not. What I fear, ranged against me, is virtue."

"You, sir, are a damnable sophist and heretic, who has learned rhetoric from Scotsmen, and sold his soul for a trifle called logic. You do not fear Satan. Pish, I say." Hargood shoveled meat into his mouth, and followed it with a gulp of wine, then glanced at his guest slyly. "Why do you not?"

"I fear above all in my opponent courage, honesty, righteousness. Why should I fear an opponent who is slothful, lazy, lost in falsehood, dissolute? Satan is not fearsome, he is pitiable. It is true, I suppose, that I would sooner treat him as a patient than ask him to dinner."

"Listening to you, sir, I believe I have already invited him to dinner. And that currently he is telling me evil does not exist."

Grange laughed aloud. "You flatter me, sir."

"Then let us return to virtue in human form. You believe at least that virtue inheres in women?"

"I believe they learn it."

"Is that why, perhaps, you form an attachment to our fine lady, Mrs. Quill? Because she is your best opponent?"

"You return constantly to a single theme, Hargood."

"I am a singular person. You have not answered my question."

"Is she my opponent?" Grange asked, rhetorically.

"She is your attachment, then."

"How do you deduce that?"

"You refute my observation?" Hargood asked.

"No, I ask you how you deduce it."

"Because you no longer speak of her. Her presence is defined, sir, by her absence in your speech."

"A pretty argument. It seems to me we have spoken several times of her."

"In diverting me from her, sir, it is you who make pretty arguments, I do protest. Each time her name is mentioned, you deflect my interest, you wax sophistical. You are like one of those saucy larks who hovers above a certain point for no reason than that his eggs are somewhere else."

Hargood wiped his mouth, leaned back in his chair, and settled his hands over his stomach, the better to study his guest. "You entertain me, though, Silas, I give you that. I do declare that I have never heard such an array of fantastical nonsense in my entire life than at a single sitting in your company."

"You shower me with praise, Hargood."

"It is no more than you deserve. We shall drink another glass, and then repair."

19

"Let us go outdoors, sir," Hargood said.

It was a habit, a form of courtesy, induced by a surfeit of
wine and the glossy condition of the night, for them to walk
out into the continual dark. They walked amiably, side by
side, beyond the circle of light where the large moths flut-
tered. There, in calm sentiment of darkness, they unburdened

and urinated on the grass edges, two physicians in confident good spirits.

The night enriched even the sounds, and the quality of their voices, just as it gave the stream, the slapping of small waves in the inlets, the splash of a fish, extra depth and density. A great gray heron, disturbed by their multiple and liquid presence, sidled bleakly upward into the air. For several seconds it hung above them, a changeable shape, resembling now a flung stone, now a hanging cross. A short while after it had dissolved into the dark, they could hear the low, calm drumbeat of its wings.

Grange finished first and buttoned his trousers. As if to demonstrate his greater virility, Hargood showered the turf with more splashing, and in his own good time adjusted his dress. Both fully buttoned, they stood for several minutes in the air, freighted with the sea's tang.

It was Hargood's habit to finish his gargantuan meal with a bowl of warm soup. It should not be hot, he claimed, for that was to give the stomach a disturbance. Warm soup settled the stomach, he was of the firm conviction, and calmed the liver.

Accordingly, Simmons was summoned from the recesses of the house to supply the final dish. With fresh bowls before them, Hargood sucked his soup for a while contentedly, before he addressed his guest again.

"I met a former colleague of yours in London, Silas, a James Granthill."

"Granthill?" Grange was momentarily surprised. "A fine student, as I recall."

Hargood sucked the soup from his spoon.

"You remember him, then?"

"Of course."

"He remembers you."

"Does he?"

Hargood paused, savoring the beef gruel, or perhaps considering his next sentence.

"He observed that in those days, when you were a student, you were something of a firebrand."

"Granthill would know about firebrands," Grange affirmed. "He was one himself."

"He said," Hargood relished the taste, "that in your quiet way, you cut quite a dash amongst the young ladies. Is that true?"

" 'Dash' is, I think, a strange word to use of me."

"Let us cut our words to suit our cloth, then. You were successful."

"Hargood, you unearth my ignoble past."

"Ignoble?"

"Irresponsible, then. Shameless. What would you prefer?"

"Never mind, sir. Wildness of heart sometimes gives rise to sanctity of mind, or so I was taught."

"A quotation?"

"A description, perhaps."

Pausing, Hargood poured a good two pinches of salt into his soup from the silver saltbowl.

"And what do you make of Granthill's evidence?" Grange asked, amused by Hargood's stolid, beavering intensity.

"What should I make of it?"

"You must decide."

"It adds another dimension to your soul, certainly."

"We speak of souls, now."

In the flickering dark, Hargood wiped his lips with his napkin, and ignored the trace of sarcasm in Grange's voice.

"You shall not put me off, dear Silas. I have the scent of something in my nostrils, and I am a very terrier when my instincts are aroused. There are two methods of keeping women at bay, as I believe. The first is to be a hellraiser or rake, the second to be a monk. It seems to me that you were once a rake, and that now you are a monk."

"A rake is not what I was."

"You were effective with women, James Granthill said, damnably effective."

"It is easy to be effective when you are young and have time on your hands, when you are not yet committed to a certain course of action, or to a career."

"You were not so studious, perhaps, as you are now."

"I have become more set in my ways, I dare think."

"Yet answer me on this matter of women. Do you not agree, there are two methods of avoidance?"

"I believe there is some truth in what you say."

"You were once a firebrand, and now you have locked yourself away."

"You circle around the facts, Hargood."

"So I do. Sniffing, testing, assessing the ground."

"And what do you find?"

"I believe you are a gray wolf, sir, on the edge of the fold."

"A wolf, is it?"

"You choose to live outside the pale of human comfort."

"Comfort and women being identical?"

"Women must be given in to in the end, Silas."

"Why so?"

"Because when we recognize women, we recognize ourselves, Silas, we recognize our souls. You will be like me. You will spend your life learning this simple fact, and in the meantime, like all other men, you will cause damage."

"If I were detached, Hargood, how might I cause damage? I am by definition neutral."

"Neutral, but not neutered, unfortunately," Hargood observed. "Don't you see how women look at you? You cause them pain. Your very presence insults them."

"You flatter me. Where are all these women? I see none of them."

"You may jest with me, sir. But it will do you no good."

"And if I were attached, assuming one such would be foolish enough to wish to attach herself to me, that would cause them less pain?"

"Pain of a different kind. Women can stand any pain from another person. What we should not do is cast them into the void."

"If I were, as you say, detached, surely it is because I have cast myself into the void, not them."

"Mere sophistry, sir. You are detached, and you must one day come into the fold."

"Perhaps we are all detached. Perhaps I merely admit it."

Hargood paused, and used the interlude to dip his bread in the last remains of soup. He chewed the bread thoughtfully, dipping it now and then. "On the contrary," he said, returning to the argument, "we are all part of the same."

"Hume says something like that. To communicate at all, we must have elements in common."

"Damn Hume, sir. That Edinburgh sophist."

"A philosopher of great acuity."

"A man who deals in opposites, in mirrors."

"He also tells us we are alone, that our internal worlds are constructed by our own internal conditions."

"Without reference to others?" Hargood asked. "He appears to give your bachelorhood an underpinning, a rationale."

"He has enlightened me, certainly, on a number of matters."

"In the process, I dare say, he has severed you from your soul."

"Hargood, sometimes you make my flesh creep a little."

"Do not take me too seriously." Hargood relented from his sport, leaning back in his chair and surveying his guest with a sideways tilt of his head that suggested affection, if not approval. "I am an old rascal."

"Speaking of severing," Hargood said suddenly, changing the subject. "What has happened to your recent amputee?"

"Swann?" Grange asked. "According to Mrs. Thompson, his shaking lasted several hours. Then he raised himself and, refusing Mrs. Thompson's help, walked home. She was concerned that he should faint, and followed behind for a hundred yards or so. But he appeared to make his way reasonably enough, and so she returned."

"He seems to have survived your handiwork, then, despite your presentiments."

"A sailor's constitution, I do believe, more than my good work. I consider he will recover."

"After a week has elapsed, you should visit him again and bleed him," Hargood opined.

"That may be so. But I do not believe in bleeding."

"Is this one of your modern fads from Edinburgh?" Hargood asked. "Bleeding has been part of the armory of the physician since classical times. Will you revoke the wisdom of tradition?"

"I prefer the rational."

"And what, pray, precisely is that?"

"It is to ask, 'What function does bleeding perform?' "

"And I say it does not matter what function it performs, if it benefits the patient."

"Does it draw off the poison? Does it resign the humors? None of these things is proved."

"It does not matter. I'll tell you what function it performs. It arrests the patient, it immobilizes him. It draws away his energy so that he sleeps. In his vitiated state he is less subject to the pain of a more energetic body. It holds him to his bed so that he does not go out and proceed to catch a chill or pneumonia, which would be more likely, in my opinion, to finish him off."

"You believe you should make him weaker so that he cannot easily arise, and cause mischief to himself?"

"Or to others. I need not remind you, sir, that a corpse is a weighty and difficult thing, and depends upon several others to move it."

"Hargood, you are, as always, a joy to behold. I only hope for my own sake that I do not fall ill under your draconian tutelage."

"I would save you, sir," Hargood assured him, "against your own will if need be."

"That, I should say, is precisely what I fear."

"Now it is you who flatter me, my dear sir. In the meantime," Hargood raised his glass, "let us drink to your good health."

"And to yours."

"In good red wine," Hargood approved.

20

*I*n his bed that night, though his mind was fuddled with too much wine, he resolved, Hargood notwithstanding, that he would carry through his agreement with Mrs. Quill to the letter, and not speak of her to anyone, except at the most superficial level and only to deflect attention. She had risked much by taking him into her confidence, and he determined to repay her for her trust in him with an absolute discretion.

That she had taken him under her wing, though her social standing was greater, had much to recommend her to him in itself. But he was increasingly convinced of a property of her character that he could only call noble, a part of her that was not so much reckless as unafraid, that he felt in due course could serve as a model, and could teach him. She impressed him in the manner in which a great animal impressed, walking backward and forward in its cage. And if this image were to be perpetuated, he felt in the same way that a keeper, sensing he is inferior to the beast that moves about inside the cage, lives cautiously on the exterior.

Now there was an added complexity. There hovered in the foreground, so to speak, the image of her daughter, who was attractive not least because she was a reflection of his patroness. He was sufficiently aware of his own feelings to believe that the daughter's beauty was enhanced by the nobility of her mother. In his mind he could not separate them, as though one were an extension of the other, or as if one flame burned within another. In the meantime, he would wait to hear from them.

The following day passed in a mild haze of activity, his appointments following one another lightly, hardly touching, yet their continuity gave him a respite from his innermost thoughts. So he proceeded through the morning and the midday, calmly allocating his time, and he would have traversed the day easily without undue commentary, except in the latter part of the afternoon when, as was his custom, he proceeded to Edred Wright's house to change his bandages.

The house—it was hardly more than a shack in which the timbers bowed outward in several places and the roof tiles were neglected—was approached through a glade of elm trees. Though it had been desolate for some time, he was struck by a sense of stillness. He knocked on the door, heard no answering call, and knocked again. Then he raised the latch and pushed the door back on its creaking hinges.

Edred Wright lay still across his bed. There is a subtle difference in attitude between sleeping and death. Grange knew precisely, as he entered the room, that what he observed was the latter. The eyes were partly open, and turned upward. There was no sign of the painful, racking breath. He appeared to have passed away peacefully during the night. A strong odor now assailed Grange, and he opened a window with difficulty in order to bring some freshness to the noxious interior.

He conducted his examination, finding no trace of struggle or violence in the expiry, and when it was completed he drew from his valise a blank death certificate. He carried with him ink in a stopper and quill pen, so that he could fill out the particulars *in situ*, while the evidence was fresh in his mind. The arrangements became the focus of his afternoon. He must pass by the Town Clerk, so that the news of the death could be posted, and, in the absence of close relatives, arrange for the funeral. He might need to pay an installment, or at least offer the undertaker a guarantee until the house was sold, and he could be paid out of the proceeds. In addition, he must inform a town lawyer who would place the proceeds in order, for almost certainly Wright had died intestate.

Thus it was not until shortly before six thirty that he arrived back at his own house, having drawn up the initial preparations. Mrs. Thompson must have been in the kitchen busy with pestle and mortar, because she did not appear to hear his knocks above the sound of her own industry. Accordingly, he withdrew a key to the house that he kept in his valise, and let himself in.

As he suspected from the rattling and clatter that came from the kitchen, interspersed with the sounds of her humming, Mrs. Thompson was engaged in her preparations for the evening meal. He was about to call out to her, to inform her of his arrival, when he observed on the sideboard a letter.

The hand was familiar. While Mrs. Thompson continued with her work in the kitchen, he opened it and read the contents carefully:

Dear Silas,

My daughter will leave shortly, two days hence on the coach. Her stay has been so short, her visit is over before it is begun.

Before she departs, we would appreciate your company, if it were possible you could afford us your time. I hope that you may be able, at such short notice, to have supper with us, poor fare though it may be, tomorrow night.

Should you be unable, as is more likely to be the case, there is no need to reply. If you are to join us, as I dearly hope, perhaps you could send a brief note ahead so that we may prepare a place.

Yours sincerely,
Celia Quill

"Mrs. Thompson!" Grange called.

Mrs. Thompson arrived flushed from her efforts in the kitchen, perspiring slightly. She had taken off her cap, whose pendants obstructed her view when she leaned forward to pound millet, and drew back an unruly strand of hair which had fallen over her cheek.

"You saw the letter, sir?"

"Thank you, yes."

"Supper at seven?"

"That would be well."

"Light," Grange spoke aloud to himself later that evening. He walked to the cupboard and opened a small wooden box. Inside it were packed, individually wrapped in brown paper, a dozen spermaceti candles. The waxy substance was the product of the cranial hollows of sperm whales. Because of its clear, steady flame, the candle was used as a standard measure for artificial light, the term "one candle power" being based on the light given by a pure spermaceti candle weighing one sixth of a pound and burning at the rate of 120 grains an hour.

Unwrapping the candle, he touched it to the flame of the tallow candle he had carried to his study. As the flax wick lit, the radiance took on a brighter quality. The two flames elided and, drawing apart, split as softly as angels. Grange allowed a drop of molten wax to fall on the base of the little, rounded iron dish. He affixed the base of the candle and held it for perhaps twenty heartbeats while it solidified and hardened.

The two candles now burned separately. While he waited, Grange studied the different sources of light. Tallow was mainly ox fat, sometimes mutton. It was yellowish, greasy, and burned with a certain amount of smoke. Yet it remained the source of illumination that was most affordable, and the commonest. The best tallow came from oxen fed on hay for a large part of the year. Even so, it was a crude mechanism. Because of its prevalence, eighteenth-century interiors were filled with the slightly rancid smell of animal fat. By comparison with the spermaceti candle, the tallow candle was a puffing engine, gathering its resources in uncertain breaths which flickered through its own shadows.

The air of the room was full of eddies. Drafts under the door rocked both flames. Licking his fingers, Grange snuffed out the wavering tallow. Now the light from the remaining spermaceti candle was purer, more constant. Over it he placed a cylindrical glass jar. The flame steadied and then rose into a simple column. There was something ecstatic in the tiny nipple or nib of light. It was a proper light to read by, a pure illumination for philosophy. He settled it on his desk and raised the source of illumination by placing it on three volumes of Aristotle's *Physicks*. Its radiance laid a soft surface on the dark wood of his desk.

Under its light Grange settled down to read from Hume's *A Treatise of Human Nature*, part 11, section 1: "Of the object and causes of love and hatred":

> *'Tis altogether impossible to give any definition of the passions of love and hatred; and that because they produce merely a simple impression, without any mixture or composition. 'Twould be as unnecessary to attempt any description of them, drawn from their nature, origin, causes and objects, and that both because these are the subjects of our present enquiry, and because these passions of themselves are sufficiently known from our common feeling and experience. This we have already observed concerning pride and humility, and here repeat it concerning love and hatred; and indeed there is so great a resemblance betwixt these two sets of passions,*

that we shall be obliged to begin with a kind of abridgement of our reasonings concerning the former, in order to explain the latter.

As the immediate object of pride and humility is self or that identical person, of whose thoughts, actions and sensations we are intimately conscious; so the object of love and hatred is some other person, of whose thoughts, actions, and sensations we are not conscious. This is sufficiently evident from experience. Our love and hatred are always directed to some sensible being external to us; and when we talk of self-love, 'tis not in a proper sense, nor has the sensation it produces anything in common with that tender emotion, which is excited by a friend or mistress. 'Tis the same case with hatred. We may be mortified by our own faults and follies; but never feel any anger or hatred, except from the injuries of others.

The pages shone against the darker background. Even behind glass, the light source which illumined this spectral interior was in constant motion. It flickered from a minuscule and hardly perceptible glimmer (while the flame seemed to hold itself to the wick by growing smaller) to a sudden flowering *lumens* as, sensing stillness, it reached upward, increasing its height and shedding a greater radiance. To a reader, this light was animate, a small living creature which crouched in semi-darkness, then sputtered and grew tall, raising the figures and shapes around it from almost dark to unexpected clarity. So the interior that it brought to his eye and then doused was not a simple one, bounded by a constant light source, but one that was in constant movement. In this flickering half-world, Grange hovered over a particular passage, and his lips murmured:

But though the object of love and hatred be always some other person, 'tis plain that the subject is not, properly speaking, the cause of these passions, or alone sufficient to excite them. For since love and hatred are directly contrary in their sensation, and have the same object in common, if that object were also their cause, it would produce the opposite reactions in equal degree; and as they must, from the very first moment, destroy each other, none of them wou'd ever be able to make its appearance. There must, therefore, be some cause different from the object.

In his concentration the surface of the page seemed like water, beneath which he peered. He shifted his position; the chair creaked; his concentration stiffened. Now the print seemed to dissolve beneath his attention, as if yielding to his eye its folds of light and denser implications. Lips parted, he whispered faintly his approval. The vellum surface gave off a faint scent of almond, intoxicating to the scholar. Hargood had said, "My dear Silas, Hume is as obscure as any mystic." Yet, Grange felt, this was also his attraction. Craned over the page, he could feel in his mind the cold wings of movement, the obscure passion of understanding, some part of him separating and lifting slowly in gray flight toward meaning.

> *For as every idea, that is distinguishable, is separable by the imagination, may be conceived to be separately existent, it is evident that the existence of one particle of matter no more implies the existence of another, than a square figure in one body implies a square figure in every one. This being granted, I now demand what results from the concurrence of* rest *and* annihilation, *and what must we conceive to follow upon the annihilation of all the air and subtle matter in the chamber, supposing the walls to remain the same, without any motion or alteration? There are some metaphysicians who answer that since matter and extension are the same, the annihilation of one necessarily implies that of the other, and there being now no distance betwixt the walls of the chamber, they touch each other, in the same manner as my hand touches the paper which is immediately before me.*

Hume focused and transfixed the mind. Sometimes Grange would return and read a passage again, so that he could gain a little more of the sense.

That night he slept unexpectedly well, whether it was in anticipation of seeing Mrs. Quill and her daughter, or the effect of a peaceful death, which reminded him of his mortality, and always, by some logic that he could not understand, had the effect of calming him.

21

"*I*f you're going out this evening, sir," Mrs. Thompson said, "it would be sensible to take a greatcoat."

She had gathered the form of her concern into a sentence, into a phrase, into a single word, that was as typical in its construction as her own physical form. For "sensible" was a word that she used as a private prerogative. In her absolute confidence of acting for his best good, it would not have occurred to her that in advising him to act "sensibly" she might be abrogating his own capacity to conduct himself in such a manner, without her prompting. Since she had committed no error, she made neither apology nor attempt at a remedy.

Yet the phrase, if it did not amuse him, unfailingly reminded him of her interest in his affairs and the claim she made over him. Since he had absurdly asked her, "Do women's souls sing?" and obtained from her an understandable and perplexed silence, he had kept quiet about all such matters relating to Mrs. Quill, except as they directly affected either his routine or her own in the running of the house.

"Will you be back this evening, sir?"

"Do not wait up for me, Mrs. Thompson. I shall take a key, and let myself in."

"Then I shall not be up if you return, sir," Mrs. Thompson said, and closed the door after him.

As he walked down the High Street, he considered the weather. Unusually, since the prevailing breeze was westerly, a cool east wind blew directly up the street toward him. Gazing upward, he saw that clouds gathered in the east over Lepe, toward Cowes, but there were no signs of the violent rainstorms that had excited the weather over the previous weeks.

Jane it was who opened the door, who took his coat and hung it under the stairs. As she faced him, smiling, and led the way to the sitting room, he noticed on her cheeks a trace of color from being exposed to the sun. It was unfashionable to be tanned, the fairest possible complexion being commonly sought, but it gave her an extra dimension of health, and he admired her all the more for flying in the face of convention—as if, in flouting the rules of beauty, she merely emphasized her own.

In the sitting room, Mrs. Quill laid down her sewing on a side table and stood up.

"Silas, it was kind of you to put aside your work."

"A pleasure, madam."

"Jane and I have spent several days in the garden. We are

becoming as strong as farm laborers. Our hands will become hard. You will no longer think us gentle."

The two women stood together and surveyed him. "Mother is mischievous," Jane said. "We enjoy our work in the garden. I have helped her to tear down old roses, and we have planted new seeds and cuttings."

"It is true. We have done more weeding in a few days together than I in a year."

"Yet your garden is always well kept, madam. I invariably feel at ease when I enter the gate and look around me, as though beauty and order always have a foothold here."

"Come, sit down."

In that same chair he remembered sitting, when they had first discussed intimacies, and she had casually impressed his heart with her courage. West-facing toward an uneasy, golden light, Mrs. Quill asked him:

"You think it will rain?"

"I cannot tell. The weather comes from the east today. There are clouds toward Southampton. From that direction it is generally unsettled."

Mrs. Quill drew her shawl more closely about her shoulders.

"You must stay the night, in any case. We could not let you wander abroad during the dark."

Jane, seated beside her on the sofa, nodded, as if in confirmation there was no need for discussion. It occurred to him then that he might mention, lightly, Mrs. Thompson's concern for his peregrinations. But he decided it would merely complicate, and instead, having prepared his housekeeper in good conscience for the eventuality of his staying out, he had not much difficulty in nodding his head in assent and thanking them for their hospitality.

At the table, it was to the topic of fashion that they turned, for Mrs. Quill had obtained a work by one Mrs. Littleton, entitled *The Fashionable Dress*, and had been intrigued by the origins of certain aspects of female and male attire.

The Rationalist

"For example," Mrs. Quill said, "white cravats worn by gentlemen, above the chin, were originally cloths twisted up and wrapped around the neck, by Croatian horsemen, to protect them from the cut of sabers."

"You do intrigue me, madam. I wear them and I did not know I was a Croatian at heart."

"Exactly so. The fashion spread to France and England. Croatia, which I understand in German is called *Krabaten*, gave its name directly to that article of dress."

"I intend to use this information shamelessly to astonish my colleague Dr. Hargood."

"You tease us, Silas. Yet did you know that our common style of hair originates from the north of France, where women gathered their hair in a knot on the top of their head to protect them from sword cuts?"

"I did not . . ."

". . . And that they allowed their hair to hang down on each side of the face, for the same reason?"

"I am surprised again. It seems to me that wherever there is a threat of violence, madam, whether from Croatian horsemen or from peasants to gentlewomen, so a new fashion is born."

"I believe you are right in your theory." Mrs. Quill smiled at him. Emboldened by her encouragement, he felt able to continue in light mood.

"We think we are assailed by French ideas, yet in practice they have exported something far more important and dangerous—namely, Fashion."

"Nothing more dangerous and disconcerting to the male sex, I agree." Mrs. Quill and her daughter laughed. "Yet perhaps you believe you are exempt from Fashion in its more extreme forms?"

"I am nervous to contradict you, madam."

"Yet one more, sir, for the pot. The shortness of men's hair, that had hitherto been worn long behind. Do you know its origin?"

"You tease me with my ignorance. Yet I am perplexed. If short hair follows the common pattern of protection, I would have thought it safer to wear long, to protect the neck from Croatian horsemen or marauding peasants as they chased one over the fields in pursuit of their liberty."

"You are closer than you think, sir. For once again, it seems, violence breeds Fashion. Mrs. Littleton informs us that in France, those who suffered by the guillotine had their hair cut off before execution. After the fall of Robespierre, to have had a relative so put to death was considered a mark of gentility. And accordingly, all who wished to be thought persons of distinction cropped their hair short at the back of their head—*à la victime*, as they called it—in remembrance of those who died."

"And I myself sit here, hair cropped *à la victime* like my fellow man, and do not know my origins."

"So," Mrs. Quill turned her face toward him fully now, with a smile in the corners of her mouth, and said: "With your hair cropped short, sir, would you call yourself a victim?"

They both observed him with a calm humor, until Grange said, "Only of your kindness, madam," and both women laughed at his sally, their musical peals echoing inside him. Shortly afterward Jane left the table, to return with the main dish, a well-cooked goose that was set out before him to carve.

They set about the slices of goose with good cheer. The two women, having gardened all day, had good appetites. Dining with them, a contentment settled on Grange, such as he had not experienced in recent days.

"Do you meet often with Dr. Hargood?" Mrs. Quill asked.

"He is exceptionally hospitable, madam."

"And lonely, when he is not in London."

"Whenever he visits London, I try to return a small part of his kindness by attending to his patients."

"He has relations in London?"

"Relations, I believe so, madam." Grange was determined to be as circumspect about the nature of Hargood's visits to London as he was about her own household to Hargood. In this, it seemed to him, there was a kind of symmetry.

"He seems knowledgeable about the London fashions," Mrs. Quill persevered. "In his occasional visits, he speaks to me on matters of dress with great acuity, and perception. I believe he receives by post the London *Courier*."

"There is a sensitive side to his nature, madam, when he is not hunting or shooting."

"I understand he shoots the occasional trespasser, too," Mrs. Quill said mischievously, referring to the incident of the Salt Officer, which was widely discussed amongst the better social circles, no doubt as an example of putting Tory principles into practice.

"In his favor," Grange replied, "I have it on good authority that he stops short of eating them."

"Well, we are glad to hear of his kinder side." Mrs. Quill smiled.

Yet he had the impression, percolating through the discussion, that she was anxious about Hargood, as if some fine sense of intuition hovered there. And though he was anxious to allay her fears, he again committed himself to revealing as little of his social life to either party as was necessary to politeness.

When they had finished the meal, Mrs. Quill said to him, "I believe you know your room by now, Silas."

"I will show him, Mother," Jane said. "As you have taught me, no man can be trusted to understand the simplest of domestic matters."

"You have instructed your daughter well," Grange said. At the bottom of the stairs, Mrs. Quill addressed him. "Sleep well, sir." She embraced him lightly and swiftly, and when she drew back he saw the briefest glance between herself and her daughter before Jane led him up the stairs, gathering the folds of her dress in one hand to avoid trampling them.

22

*G*range remembered the next part as dream, as if some vapor of reality had been removed and only the pure light remained. Carrying a three-branched candelabra, Jane led him up the stairs and along the corridor to his room, standing aside at the doorway so that he could enter. As he bowed and passed her, she bestowed upon him a smile both direct and distant. He was reminded of truth, escaping by a side door.

"Good night, Silas."

"Good night, Jane." Grange paused. "I will see you before you go tomorrow?"

"If you should wish it."

In some private aspect of himself, he realized what she was offering, though his mind considered it obliquely. He viewed the thought only in profile, as if half its face were in shadow. Yet the course of life is sometimes decided in half-seconds. Inside him he sensed some movement of his soul, some vestige of courage or terror which enabled him to turn to her full face, direct.

"I do wish it."

With the trace of a smile, she held out the candelabra to him, so that he could take it to light his room: "I know this house, I can find my way."

He watched until the glimmer of her dress had disappeared. A faint *lumens* of light in the stairwell came from beneath stairs.

Mrs. Quill's footsteps moved below. Grange fancied he could hear her walk into the hallway and bolt the front door of the house. He closed the door behind him and stood for what seemed several minutes with the candleflames flickering independently in his hand. He was aware of time passing, even though time, the time of the mind, is like a kind of denseness that is not measurable. A short while later he crossed to the bed. A nightshirt had been laid across it. He set down the candelabra on the sideboard.

Undressing slowly, he removed his dark, formal clothes. As he undressed, he laid each garment over a chair, until its stiff frame, piled with clothes, seemed a scarecrow. Naked, he was briefly illuminated by the faint candlelight. Yet it was as if his body was revealed to him for the first time. He put on the nightshirt and took to the bed, drawing the sheets up over him.

For several minutes, or longer, he lay facing the ceiling, considering what had been said. The shadows edged back and forth across the room with the movements of the candleflames. He stared contemplatively into the dark, imposing upon it vague notions and fancies which, hardly formed, drifted away to be replaced by others.

How long before he heard the faint brush of cloth against the outside door, and the handle turned quietly? A figure entered in a long, white shift and gracefully pivoted to close the door. Staring at the ceiling, he was only aware of her as a presence. The door closed soundlessly. She carried no light. Aware of the turning swirl of a white nightdress, for a brief moment Grange was not certain of her identity. Something in his heart stood still while she crossed the floor and stood above his bed. There, Jane gazed down at him through the lake of his thoughts. He looked up at her, into her steady gaze. She raised her shift, then her naked body joined him beneath the sheets.

Mrs. Thompson's room was quiet, filled with deep breathing, then odd gasps. After a few minutes, she settled into loud snoring. Her plump hand resided on the chair. She continued to snore deeply. Some scene was being enacted, a conversation between two people, a man and a woman, thoughts rising from the dark of contemplation. Yet she could not hear what they were saying. The language was familiar yet imprecise, as though meaning were carried by tone and inflection rather than the words themselves.

Not long afterward, Mrs. Thompson opened her eyes, suddenly awake. Her fingers had released the napkin, which had fallen to the floor. She heaved herself up, glanced at the clock, which read two in the morning, blinked with surprise, lit a candle and, sighing deeply, removed herself to her bedroom.

At early dawn, Grange woke. Morning light streamed through the window. He screwed up his eyes against the brightness.

The other side of the bed was empty. In consternation, he raised himself on an elbow.

"Jane?" he asked, as if she might emerge from the corners of the room. There was a trace of warmth where she had lain sleeping, an impression as faint as a ghost.

Noticing her shift had gone too, he rose from the bed and began hurriedly to dress, standing on the cold floor and fumbling with his buttons. Emerging into the formality of clothes, he walked along the corridor, down the stairs into the hall.

The figure of a woman crossed the room ahead of him. Mrs. Quill turned toward him.

"You slept well?"

"Yes . . ."

Her gray eyes studied him. He sensed in their interior a calm goodwill, though perhaps some brief surprise at seeing him so suddenly, unannounced. Perhaps she noticed his agitation, but if she did so, her message was delivered implacably. "Jane left at dawn. She has to travel to Winchester by early stage."

A terrible fear quickened through Grange. Noticing his commotion, Mrs. Quill picked up a letter from a sideboard.

"She asked me to give you this."

Though Grange was given naturally to formality, he hardly restrained himself from seizing it.

"Thank you."

"Would you like breakfast?"

"I would indeed. You are most kind."

Mrs. Quill looked at him once again, a calm stare with neither approval nor disapproval, but taking in perhaps his condition.

"I will let you in peace to read."

She disappeared into the kitchen. Grange tore open the letter and read under his breath.

Dear Silas,
I leave early for the coach which departs for Southampton, and then to Winchester. With pain in my heart I return to my life and

my responsibilities. I will remember your kindness for the rest of my days.

I remain yours,
Jane

A physical aggravation began to hammer behind his eye. He stepped backward so that he could lean against the sideboard, and heard Mrs. Quill emerge behind him. She began to place, calmly and in deliberate sequence, condiments on the table. Swallowing, he hastily slipped the letter into his pocket.

Mrs. Quill, as always the good hostess, waited for him at the breakfast table. Gathering himself, Grange traversed the short distance to the table without mishap, and sat down. There was no sign of enquiry in the glance she gave him. He strained his entire system to appear calm.

"Do you take tea?"

"Please."

She poured carefully. He observed the flight of the liquid.

"You seem caught up in thought, Silas."

"It is true I am struck with thought."

Mrs. Quill placed a cup beside him.

"If we're to collaborate, you must let me be your confidante."

"You are right, madam."

Grange could restrain himself no further. He breathed out: "I am arrested by contemplation."

Mrs. Quill, softly: "Contemplation of departure?"

"My reticence embarrasses me."

Mrs. Quill's hand reached out across the table and her hand settled on his. Grange looked down at this amicable relation, one hand covering another.

"May I speak?" Mrs. Quill asked.

Grange nodded.

"We agreed on a plan, Silas. You have behaved most excellently. I spoke of sleeping women, and you have already awakened one"—she paused—"who left this morning with her soul alight, whom I had to pack onto the coach in case she bolted back to you." It seemed to Grange that she was talking with great deliberation, that he could not see her for her voice. "My daughter is married. She is a good wife and I wish her well. Her husband is an excellent match—prosperous and . . . tolerant. I do not know what you intend, but it is not, nor was not, my intention to disturb their peace and harmony."

For the first time, it seemed to him, he observed Mrs. Quill's true strength of character, her ruthlessness in action, and for several seconds in consideration of this he was lost for words.

Mrs. Quill withdrew her hand from his, and sipped her tea.

"You meant me to wake her, madam?"

"Wake her?" She replaced the cup. "Yes. I meant it so."

"Then you sent her away, out of danger."

His heart hammered again.

"She is in love." Stated so implacably, he wondered again at her strength. "At least, sir, she thinks she is. In that state, she should be sent away. Given time, I have no doubt that she will get over it."

"Madam, this frightens me. You are playing with lives."

Perhaps she would respond. Yet he noticed no hesitation in her eyes, merely a calm pause for emphasis.

"Silas, it is your very innocence which causes you pain, and which perhaps causes her to think she loves you. I merely remind you of our agreement."

"Innocence?" Grange asked, as if speaking of another man. "I am a doctor of thirty-seven years, having seen something of life . . ."

"Innocence, sir, is a state of mind."

"Madam?"

"It has nothing to do with experience, or age."

He tried to bring his mind to practicalities. In his agitation, he could be certain of only one thing, that no amount of discussion would dissuade Mrs. Quill from her chosen path. He was a rationalist; he must accept such truths.

"Madam, I thank you for your hospitality. You have given me much to think about. I too must return to my responsibilities."

Mrs. Quill rose.

"Goodbye, Silas."

She led the way to the door, opened it, stood aside to let him pass.

"Good-day, madam."

"Good-day."

She closed the door behind him. He walked fast down the path to the gate, opened it, then continued down the lane.

Mrs. Thompson swung the door, staring at him.

"Good morning, Mrs. Thompson."

Grange strode past her. She followed him.

"Do you require breakfast, sir?"

Grange turned to face her.

"No, I have eaten, thank you."

Mrs. Thompson looked him up and down.

"Are you well, sir?"

Realizing how odd his behavior must appear, Grange made a conscious effort to deflect her questioning.

"Do I seem unwell?"

Mrs. Thompson's expression was equivocal.

"I suppose I must seem so." He changed the subject. "I have an appointment at nine, I think. I must check my diary."

"Sir, Mr. Collier has been waiting for a quarter of an hour."

"I will wash my face and hands. Send him in in five minutes."

Mrs. Thompson, though still dubious about his behavior, nodded and left. Grange ascended the stairs to his study.

Once he had reached his sanctuary, Grange poured a jug of water into the bowl and washed his face. He shaved himself, rinsed and dried his face. Even to his own eyes, glancing in the mirror, perplexity inhabited the corners of his face. He sat down at his desk. Announcing herself by a single knock, Mrs. Thompson put her face around the door.

"Mr. Collier, sir."

Grange, standing, said, "My apologies for being late, sir. Please sit down."

Throughout the morning he performed his rites, while feeling strangely out of body. Rising and sinking in his chair, uttering greetings, offering advice, he heard himself speak as if from a distance, as if he seemed other than himself. The rites continued until, at the end of the day, he sat forward in his chair, his face in his hands. Mrs. Thompson found him and, seeing him, halted.

"Are you sure you're well, sir?"

Startled, Grange raised his face from his hands, attempting to recover his composure.

"A little tired, perhaps."

"It's nearly five o'clock. Would you like some tea, sir?"

Grange smiled. "Thank you."

With a final glance at him, Mrs. Thompson left.

When he was sure she had departed, Grange reached for paper, dipped a pen in ink, and began to write.

> *Dear Mrs. Quill,*
>
> *I thank you most earnestly for your hospitality, and for the opportunity to meet your daughter Jane.*
>
> *In view of the inclement weather, it was most considerate of you to allow me to stay overnight.*
>
> *At the risk of repeating my error of judgment, I apologize for my shortness at the breakfast table this morning, and beg your forgiveness for my ill-considered words.*
>
> *In all things about which we have spoken, you have made your position clear, and in all spoken matters you have kept your word.*
>
> *In gratitude and good wishes, I thank you for your kindness, and remain most sincerely yours,*
>
> *Silas Grange*

He blotted the letter. A shuffle of skirts indicated Mrs. Thompson ascending the stairs. Briskly, Grange placed the letter in the drawer. Mrs. Thompson entered with a tray, a kettle, cup and saucer. He watched her place the tray on the desk.

"Thank you," Grange said. "I'll pour it myself."

"You'll have dinner here tonight, sir?"

"Please. I'll go for my customary walk and will be back by six thirty."

Mrs. Thompson gave him a final, penetrating glance and left.

Grange opened the drawer, withdrew the letter, placed it in an envelope, put the envelope in his coat pocket, and rose to take his constitutional.

23

*K*eeping to unpopulated footpaths, Grange reached Mrs. Quill's house, opened the gate, and walked up the pathway. The garden had a chill silence. He slipped the letter under the door and returned down the footpath, closing the gate behind him.

The posting of the letter released him. Outside, an impression of concern seemed to leave him. He counseled patience and began to breathe deeply of the sea air. Physical activity freshened the mind. He began to walk along the Walhampton foreshore with a brisk stride. Nature distracted him. Clouds rose above the Solent and formed a tablecloth over the higher hills of the Isle of Wight. He strode along in the fresh air, following the shoreline, swinging his cane. Reaching the edge of the water, he paused and stared out over the marshes to the sea.

For the first time that day he had lost the sense of panic which had haunted him. If he were patient enough, he was certain that he would meet Jane again. He must immerse himself in other matters, and fate would provide his chance.

Vague lights rose from the surface of the inland estuaries. Clouds of gulls seemed specks of light. Beyond Jack-in-the-Basket a dark raft of waterbirds rose and fell on the glassy swell.

Mrs. Thompson opened the door. Grange removed his boots and she handed him his undershoes.

"Thank you, Mrs. Thompson. I will be in my study."

"You'll be looking forward to your dinner, sir." She stood aside to let him pass, though beneath her eyelids she watched him carefully.

"I shall indeed."

"Then I'll call you down in half an hour."

Closing the door, Mrs. Thompson disappeared into the interior. Grange ascended the stairs to his study. Removing from the bookshelf *A Treatise of Human Nature*, he placed it on the desk, opened it at a place marked with a slip of paper, and began to read:

> *We must therefore glean up our experiments in this science from a cautious observation of human life, and take them as they appear in the common course of the world, by men's behaviour in company, in affairs, and in their pleasures. Where experiments of this kind are judiciously collected and compared, we may hope to establish on them a science which will not be inferior in certainty, and*

will be much superior in utility, to any other of human com-
prehension. . . .

At table, though, eating his supper, Grange was clearly immersed in thought. The weather had changed again, from
almost clear skies to a fickle overcast, which dropped brief
attenuated showers and produced odd breezes. Mrs. Thompson drifted around him like a concerned cloud.

He rose from table, proceeding upstairs to his study, settled
himself at table, opened again *A Treatise of Human Nature*, and
began again to read to himself:

Thus, in sleep, in a fever, in madness, or in any very violent
emotions of soul, our ideas may approach our impressions: as on the
other hand it sometimes happens, that our impressions are so faint
and low, that we cannot distinguish them from our ideas. . . .

The weather of his soul had not changed that night, when he
lay in bed, staring at the ceiling. Some aspect of thought
oppressed him, though he could not identify the source of his
foreboding. It was part of his philosophy, one of his rules of
life, to allow only that which was identifiable to be admitted
into reason. Yet when he closed his eyes, the same thoughts
haunted him. He tried to put away the thought of Jane, but
that night he was subject to a very violent and lucid imagin-
ing, which caused him to lie awake, sweating, until an interval
of time reduced its vehemence.

On principle, he did not take account of dreams. A dream
was nothing more than a vague fancy or intuition. The sensations and outlines that it conjured were of no more interest
than the arbitrary shapes of steam rising above water. As
such, it could take on the aspect of a shape here, suggest
something else there, but one might as well search for the
rules of the Euclidean geometry in the leaves of a teacup. So

that when he woke up in the morning, and a sustained, pure light poured on his face, he could put aside his imaginings with nothing more than a shudder, and raise himself with a certain fortitude to meet the day.

When, dressed, Grange descended to breakfast, Mrs. Thompson, standing in the hallway, announced:

"A letter for you, sir."

She held it out to him, and he was obliged to step forward to take it. He had a suspicion she watched him as he reached for it.

"Thank you, Mrs. Thompson."

Having briefly considered his appearance, Mrs. Thompson nodded and departed. He counted fully thirty seconds before he opened the envelope.

> *Dear Silas,*
>
> *You need not apologize to me for a small and temporary loss of your customary charm. I feel I know you well enough already that I understand you. I shall write no more on this except to say that no forgiveness is needed.*
>
> *Jane will come again in a few weeks' time, perhaps. When she does I will ask you again to dinner.*
>
> *I received a letter from her today, from which I deduce she has recovered somewhat her composure. Taking a favorable view of her recuperation in a few weeks, I have no objection to her meeting you again.*
>
> *In the meantime, I should like much to see you again.*
>
> *For the time being I shall, however, be away for several days. I wonder whether Friday will suit you to join me and two old friends of mine for dinner?*
>
> *I remain, yours sincerely,*
> *Celia Quill*

Having read the letter a second time, Grange folded it and placed it in his pocket. He would have paused to consider the matter further, several of its implications being uncertain, but a few seconds later with a sound of brisk footsteps Mrs.

Thompson appeared and her presence broke into his thoughts.

"Breakfast, sir?"

"Thank you."

Still in thought, he walked to the window and peered briefly out. The sky was overcast today as yesterday, and the atmosphere seemed weighted. There was a glare upon the surface of the Solent. Sometimes the Lymington air appeared soft and dense, as if it had itself recently woken, spreading either lassitude or contentment. There was, in polite circles, much discussion of its properties. Some thought the atmosphere beneficial, that it calmed the soul and thereby (so it was argued) caused a contented and a longer life; others that it acted as a brake upon the spirits, like some anesthetic or drug, from which it was difficult to awaken. These two sides both gave as their opinion that the quantity of moisture in the sea air was the cause of these properties, beneficent or otherwise.

He sat down at the dining table, and for several minutes absentmindedly moved the condiments back and forth across the surface of the tablecloth, forming now a line, now a triangle. He was thus engaged when Mrs. Thompson reentered, carrying ham and bread.

So he immersed himself in routine, though he seemed strangely detached from it; whether it was in his surgery, advising patients with professional confidence on the conduct of their affairs, or later, walking along the foreshore, lost in his thoughts, striding forward; or in his study, reading *A Treatise of Human Nature*, poring over the pages. Something, some unresolved aspect, seemed to stand between him and what he did.

Friday came. Showing out a patient at the end of another day's work, Grange closed the door, leaned against it with some relief, considering, and was immersed for several minutes in his thoughts until Mrs. Thompson broke in on his reverie by knocking on the outside of the door, and called to him:

"Will you be here for supper this evening, sir?"

"No, Mrs. Thompson. I shall be out to dinner."

A pause on the other side of the door, a brief cough, a careful silence.

"Or breakfast, sir?"

The question struck home, causing him to pause, even to shake free of his thoughts, for it made him, usually well in control of his responses and confident of his position, realize suddenly how closely Mrs. Thompson was following his movements.

"If it does not rain, Mrs. Thompson."

"Very good, sir."

Mrs. Thompson's steps hesitated on the landing briefly, as if judging for herself the quality of his response, then descended. For several seconds he listened after her, both annoyed by and admiring of her percipience, before he pushed himself away from the door, walked to the other side of his study, and sat down again at his desk.

24

Approaching the house on a midsummer evening, the Solent was covered in a graceful cloud, light rising from the surface of the sea. The lightest of breezes caused ripples to sound on the wooden piles along the foreshore. Grange experienced a moment of completion. He had set on his best coat, which though not of London cut, was serviceable, and a Malacca cane. Approaching Mrs. Quill's house, he noticed in the adjacent yard a handsome brougham with two horses, the horses unyoked and set into a nearby field, and a saddleboy sitting chewing a piece of grass. The bronze knocker struck a solid note.

Mrs. Quill opened the door.

"Silas."

Grange doffed his wide-brimmed hat. "It is a pleasure to see you again, madam."

"Come through, sir."

Following Mrs. Quill to the sitting room, Grange experienced again that familiar lightness of being which seemed to accompany him in her presence. Perhaps the brightness of the summer evening had settled his senses. Yet, for whatever reason, the very air appeared charged with scent and silks. Mrs. Quill's stately back preceded him through the hallway and toward the sitting room.

Entering, he observed two women seated, and was subject to that remote chill of fear and perhaps exhilaration which greets new and unknown arrivals. Having brought him into the room, Mrs. Quill stood aside so that Grange could advance and the two women rose to greet him. In retrospect he would remember that first impressions left their indelible mark, that confidence in women is like power in men; it holds and impresses. He guessed their ages to be both in their forties, more handsome perhaps than pretty. Though Grange was not a man much given to the study of fashion, either generally or in detail, even so he found himself affected by the sense of dress, the impression of elegance, which seemed to form naturally around them. And even his lack of interest in fashion could not prevent him from noticing that the three women were an uncommon sight of refinement. If there was ever a revolution in women's dress, it was occurring now. The panniers and complexities had disappeared in favor of a simple elegance of line, in a change of styles whose extent had never before been equaled.

"Mrs. Angela Boxer . . . Dr. Silas Grange."

Mrs. Boxer wore a dress of Spitalfields silk, her dark curls offset by the cream of her dress. She extended a hand bereft of all ornaments except a single ring, and studied him with detachment as he kissed her hand. Mrs. Pugh, the other guest, was a woman of some bearing who advanced toward him with stately grace. And Mrs. Quill, set between these her companions, stood back, smiling at the impressionable guest.

"Mrs. Arabella Pugh . . . Dr. Silas Grange."

"How do you do, madam."

The introductions over, the party sat down in a drawing room which, overlooking the river, seemed to take reflection from its pallid surface and now brimmed with a soft, golden light.

Mrs. Quill began to speak. "Silas, Mrs. Pugh is the wife of James Morecambe Pugh, the owner of mines. Mrs. Pugh lives at Downton, near Salisbury."

"I travel by the village sometimes," Grange said, "on my way to Salisbury."

"You have an interest in that city?" Mrs. Pugh asked.

"My idea of a holiday, madam, and a refreshment of my poor soul, is to listen to the choir of Salisbury Cathedral singing Thomas Tallis."

"You are devout, doctor?"

"No, and that is my guilt. I love church music but am not myself devout."

"Yet you travel to Salisbury to listen to sacred music?"

"In the matter of Tallis, I would compare myself to a humble dog who listens to his master singing and sometimes joins in with the occasional howl."

The three women laughed. It was a note well struck. Yet Mrs. Boxer had a notion to pursue it.

"Yet it is a journey of some four hours?"

"Six hours by coach, madam. If I leave at five in the morning, I am there in time for the late morning service."

"And you return the same day?"

"As often as not."

"That is twelve hours of travel to listen to a single service. I commend your singleness of purpose, sir, for a dog who must needs howl."

In similar light banter they spent perhaps a half hour, while he observed, behind Mrs. Quill and through the window, the sun setting golden behind Lymington Hill and, as dusk drew on, a chill movement of light above the waters of the river.

At table, Mrs. Quill sat at one end, Grange at the other, the two women in the middle. For several seconds they continued to talk, but in one part of his mind Grange did not hear them, for he was taken with the notion that this was where Jane sat, on another evening that seemed to press forward in his imagination. He was engaged in these thoughts, until he realized that his attention had quite slipped away, and that Mrs. Pugh was leaning toward him to make a point.

"I have a small house and estate, the running of which is taken care of by my bailiff, Mr. Frear."

"Small?" repeated Mrs. Boxer. "My dear Dr. Grange, she owns half the land in Wiltshire."

"You exaggerate, I do believe," Mrs. Pugh riposted. "It has certain advantages, but it is far from London. Perhaps, Dr. Grange, you will do me the kindness of a visit—that is, when you can get away from the attentions of your grateful patients?"

"Thank you. Perhaps, if time permits."

Mrs. Pugh to Mrs. Quill: "Celia, cannot you persuade this most charming man to visit me?"

Mrs. Quill smiled. Mrs. Boxer interceded:

"Arabella, you have no ailment for the young doctor to cure, except perhaps boredom."

Good-natured, Mrs. Pugh replied: "You are thoroughly cruel, Angela. And you, I think, have no ailment except a husband."

"I would refute you, Arabella, excepting only what you say is true."

There was general laughter amongst the ladies. Grange smiled, though a little distractedly. Occasionally he glanced down the table at Mrs. Quill, sitting composed. Several times Mrs. Quill glanced briefly at him, and once or twice gave him a charming smile. He smiled back.

Later in the evening, all parties having had a certain amount to drink, a matter which was reflected in their animation and increased intimacy, they repaired again to the sitting room, where candles had been lit by Mrs. Quill's maid.

". . . So," Mrs. Boxer continued, "I said to my husband, 'My dear James, there is little that I will not allow you to do in this house, but to bring your horse into the kitchen with your drunken friends is too much.' My husband knows no culture, my good doctor, except what he picks up in London."

Laughter from the other two women.

Late in the evening, Grange toyed with his glass.

Mrs. Quill announced, "Silas seems tired after his week."

"I apologize if I tire in such enjoyable company. Perhaps it is time I made my way home."

"It was most kind of you to join us."

"Forgive me, madam, if I take my leave."

"Goodbye." Mrs. Pugh placed a scented hand on his arm. "I hope that one day we shall see you again."

Grange offered his courteous goodbyes. Mrs. Quill followed him to the hall. In the hallway she removed his coat from the cupboard, and insisted that he turn around so that she could place the garment over his shoulder. It was a heavy coat, and raising it he heard at his ear the expulsion of effort in her breath. As her hand touched him, he experienced an involuntary shudder like fear, that seemed to drive downward, as if he might have been a horse nervous of human contact, or as though his body responded to something that his mind did not.

"Goodbye, Silas. Thank you for a most pleasant evening."

"Goodbye, madam. Perhaps you will convey my respects to Jane."

"Perhaps."

Having helped him with his coat, she handed him his hat and cane.

She opened the door and Grange stepped outside.

From the doorway, Mrs. Quill said: "You would not like a lamp to light your way?"

"No, thank you. I am used to making my way at night. It is necessary on my rounds."

"Are you sure?"

"Certain, I assure you, madam."

"Then goodbye, sir."

The door closed, and he turned away.

There was sufficient moonlight to see by. The garden seemed to breathe sweet scents. When he reached the gate that led to the road, he noticed no signs of the broughams, horses, or grooms, and assumed that they had adopted the practice of proceeding to a local inn overnight, where the horses could be stabled and the grooms themselves could be housed in cheap accommodation, before calling for their mistresses in the morning.

On the road that ran parallel he could hear curlews, the lap of water, and the call of a nightjar. In reasonable spirits, he began to walk back to his house.

25

*I*t was on his way to breakfast, pausing to adjust his coat, that Grange observed an envelope left on the sideboard by Mrs. Thompson. It was the creamy vellum that Mrs. Quill used, the address in long strokes. A form of anticipation, or apprehension, passed through him as he recognized the writing. Concentration had a way of stilling the mind. He paused above the sideboard, raised the letter and, as he opened it, caught the faintest trace of scent that issued from its surfaces.

> *My dear Silas,*
>   *It was gratifying to see you in such good health.*
>   *You made a fine impression on my guests. I received a letter from Mrs. Pugh, asking me to forward the enclosed invitation to you.*
>   *I hope that you will accept. She likes you much. If you do so, and thus show yourself outgoing, and unaffected by infatuation with my daughter, I shall assume that you are better disposed to meet Jane again.*
>   *My warmest wishes,*
>   *Celia Quill*

The letter struck him with intense thought, causing his spirits first to lift and hover, and then to fall, in such close conjunction and with such speed that his emotions seemed to occur all at once, an unlikely animation. He heard Mrs. Thompson approach and slipped the letter into his pocket.

"Mrs. Thompson, I shall require no breakfast this morning. It is half an hour before my first appointment. You may be assured that I will return by then."

"Yes, sir."

Outside, the summer sun was already warm. In the pervasive stillness, he could hear bees and birdsong from the gardens which lay behind the ostlery. Grange closed the door and made his way down the High Street toward the bridge. Crossing it, he began to walk up the hill toward Mrs. Quill's house. He turned a corner and in due course pressed on the gate of her garden. It opened with a creak. He swung it briskly behind him and walked up the pathway to the front door. In the shadow of the entrance portico, he knocked and waited.

Eventually bolts were slid and the door was opened. Mrs. Quill appeared as if dressed to go out. She wore a heavy cloak, a bonnet, and a basket was set down on the floor beside her.

"Why, Silas, this is an unexpected pleasure."

"May I speak with you, madam?"

"Certainly," Mrs. Quill replied. After a brief pause, she added: "Come inside."

In the hallway she turned to face him. Out of courtesy, perhaps as much as hesitation, several seconds passed before he could speak.

"Madam, I seek to clarify your recent letter to me."

"Oh?" A faint hint of raised eyebrow; a cool gaze.

"If I understand your import, the possibility of my seeing your daughter Jane again is conditional upon my paying a social visit to Mrs. Pugh."

What did he observe behind her eyes, so calmly studying him? The implication that she could see into his mind, that she knew him better than he did himself? He watched the words frame themselves on her lips. "Silas, my import is for you to decide. I wrote my letter in good faith."

"I see." He experienced the flood of concern and suspicion that he had, until now, held back. "That is your last word?"

There was, by contrast, no trace of suspicion or concern on Mrs. Quill's own face, merely an expression of clarity and clear direction.

"It is, on that subject, my last word."

He had read of the literary metaphors of the heart, yet for a few seconds now he experienced a kind of breathlessness, and he fancied he could hear the echo of his own heart's faint pulsing in his temples, like one of those flies or trapped insects that struggles against a windowpane.

"Thank you. I will trouble you no further. Good-day, madam. I apologize for inconveniencing you, and will return now to my work."

As her guest, he should perhaps have waited for her to open the door. But in his emotion he himself turned and had gripped the handle and engaged it, when she spoke calmly but firmly behind him.

"Silas."

He was already on a course, pressing down the handle and opening the door, but in the open doorway he turned round reluctantly, and paused. Mrs. Quill drew closer.

"You are too hasty, Silas, in your assumptions."

He felt, again, the sensation of his heart beating.

"My assumptions, madam, are that you are maneuvering me."

"Maneuvering?" She herself stood unmoving in the hallway. In opening the door, he had been struck again by sunlight. Looking back into the interior, his eyes still filled with brightness, he could make out her figure, but not her expression. Her words floated toward him from the shadow of her face. "You and I made an agreement upon a certain course of action."

Readjusting to the dimness of the light, under his eyes her features slowly re-formed.

"And I say I have not the stomach for it."

"I see." Mrs. Quill nodded, and as if to confirm it to herself she nodded again. "So be it."

"So be it," he repeated.

"Good-day, sir."

"Good-day, madam."

He backed outward from the doorway. Mrs. Quill came forward calmly to close it. In that final gesture of foreclosure his heart seemed to jump like a frightened rabbit. Even in adversity, there was something resolute and fine about her self-control. The door closed. Grange turned and walked down the garden path. He swung the garden gate behind him and chose, almost without thinking, a path that would take him back along the foreshore.

The water had the effect of magnifying the light. Strange hopes and fears rose inside him like birds, but he would hold them at bay. He would dissolve them in his work, and allow his shattered equanimity to recover. Yet some thought held him back.

Was he being mischievous? Had he broken a promise? The thought troubled him as he paused at the water's edge. Further out, toward Jack-in-the-Basket, fisher boats drifted on the calm surface. Already the sun was hot, and now its flames appeared to reach up to him from the water itself. He peered into the dazzling surface with an intensity of longing, and for a moment it seemed he was staring into a chasm of meaninglessness where everything was nameless and without relation. His heart pounding, sharing in the vertigo of water, he viewed a world of superstition, of unspoken fears, a world of wood spirits, angels, mediums. Throughout his life he had attempted, by his regime, to protect himself from precisely these sensations of chaos; now he knew he risked falling prey to that intensity of emotion which is like madness.

By overcoming an indefinable terror he brought himself to the edge, into its nacreous fires, and rather than falling, his fear and anguish rose up toward him. For a brief moment he heard inside himself the cry of someone in frustration, a sound such as he had heard one afternoon walking by the Mortlake. Yet the expression of that rage, savage and extreme, now falling inside him like an echo, brought him something like respite, if not peace. The water resolved again into its surface. It supported again the fishing boats and his world. He felt faint briefly, but after a few seconds was able to move on.

Mrs. Thompson met him at the door.

"Give me five minutes, Mrs. Thompson," Grange said, "then send in the first patient."

Under her appraising eyes, he walked upstairs and crossed the landing. Outside her purview, he slumped into his chair, and once more, like a fisherman peering into the water, he stared for several minutes into the polished surface of his desk.

It was another day. A dozen ailments whose causes were obscure. Stomach gripe, headaches, the product of a thousand causes, from bad meat to tainted water. The patients not only had physical symptoms but came to him with their own preferred versions of the causes, so that he must not only attempt to find the real causes, but navigate between the prejudices of his patients like a pilot between sandbars, attempting at one and the same time to gently dissuade them from their superstitions and old wives' tales, and to provide a remedy. He was sometimes ruefully reminded of the saying of a certain Dr.

Johnson to the effect that the function of the physician is to entertain the patient while nature effects the cure.

As it happened, amongst the more usual complaints, there was a casualty from one of the sawpits at Buckler's Hard. Nearly halfway through the morning, at not long after eleven o'clock, a horse and litter approached the front door. There was a loud knock, and he heard further sounds from the hallway. Mrs. Thompson's voice gave brisk instructions to another man as they helped to unhitch the litter and carry the unfortunate victim into the house. Grange was hardly finished examining a patient for jawache, and was just then proceeding to the stand to wash his hands, when he was called upon by Mrs. Thompson standing at the bottom of the stairwell.

Detecting some urgency in her voice, he crossed the landing and walked down the stairs. The litter lay along the floor. Mrs. Thompson had fetched a glass of water and was holding up the patient's head with one hand so that he could drink. His teeth chattered so much from fever it seemed he would break the glass. His companion, a drover, stood against the wall, wiping the sweat from his face with his shirtsleeve. Since Grange wished no further witnesses to any operation than were absolutely necessary, he was at pains to dismiss the wounded man's accomplice.

To the sweating drover, he said, "You have done well. He is now with us. You should return, if you would, in an hour."

The drover nodded and left.

The blanket covering the patient had been drawn back. Across his abdomen was a huge gash, and the signs of a terrible sawtooth. As if by good fortune, the cavity of the abdomen had not been punctured so badly that the insides had gushed out. A rudimentary stitching had taken place, perhaps by some canvasmaker or sailstitcher. In the extremity of his anguish, Grange found these external wounds, whose cause was plain and whose treatment was not in doubt, strangely welcome to his mind. Nothing is better for dealing with one crisis than to have it dissolved by a greater and more pressing one.

There was nothing he could do but attempt to make a neater

work of the stitching. He set about it immediately he had drawn his conclusions.

To Mrs. Thompson he said, "Vinegar, astringent, if you please. And rum."

"Sir."

"And a piece of cloth, to bite on."

Mrs. Thompson left for the storeroom.

"Can you speak?"

He received in turn a movement of lips, and then a ghastly, but competent, smile.

Mrs. Thompson raised the patient's head again for the rum. While the man absorbed the shock of the spirit Mrs. Thompson poured down his throat, Grange applied astringent to the wound. He would sew part of the gash before releasing the existing few stitches, like scaffolding that had done its purpose. Mrs. Thompson distracted the patient with further rum while Grange began to sew the lips of the wound together. Sometimes the muscles of the shipwright's stomach bulged with pain, and Grange was forced to wait until the spasm relaxed before using the needle again. Once or twice, in these muscular contractions, the lining of the stomach appeared beneath the lips of the wound, and he sewed carefully from one end and then the other until the stitches in the middle could be released. By then the patient had fainted, and he could continue in silence.

When he had finished, Mrs. Thompson and he carried the litter through to the utility room, where she made up a bed, and they put him to temporary rest. There Grange applied vinegar again, and put on dressings, and by the time the process was finished and the man could be left, it was time for lunch.

Not long afterward, Mrs. Thompson informed him that the drover had returned.

"Tell him we will keep the patient overnight, and that we will arrange to take him home by brougham."

"Yes, sir."

"Mrs. Thompson?"

"Sir?"

"Give the man a shilling for transporting the patient to us."

"He didn't do it for money, sir. There's no need . . ."

"A shilling, please. And my good wishes. Perhaps he will bring other patients to us."

Mrs. Thompson understood pecuniary motives, and nodded.

"Sir."

In the afternoon, between further consultations, he went down several times to check his patient's condition. The fever was still upon him, but now he had woken. Lying on his back, he breathed deeply, though not without difficulty. Mrs. Thompson had brought up a chair and sat sewing beside him. She nodded to Grange to signify the patient was in a peaceful condition, and whispered: "I will call you if he needs attention, sir." Relieved, Grange returned to his study to call in the next patient.

"Goodbye, Mrs. Dawkins," he said to the final visitor of the afternoon. "Take care of yourself. No exercise, plenty of rest."

At Mrs. Dawkins's leaving, Grange closed the door and returned to his desk, then drew a sheet of paper toward him and began to write:

> *Dear Mrs. Pugh,*
> *I thank you for your invitation to visit you.*
> *I would be pleased to take up your kind offer as it may suit you. Since I am at regular work on five days of the week, perhaps you would consider whether a Saturday would be convenient to pay my respects.*
> *Yours sincerely,*
> *Silas Grange*

He folded the letter, placed it in an envelope, and put it in his desk. Then he stood up, drew down *A Treatise of Human Nature*, and began to read:

> *That we may understand the full extent of these relations, we must consider, that two objects are connected together in the imagination,*

not only when the one is immediately resembling, contiguous to, or the cause of the other, but also when there is interposed between them a third object, which bears to both of them any of these relations. . . .

So he continued, tired from his day's work, though his mind and emotions were temporarily at rest, or at least absorbed, and grateful for other distractions.

26

The following day, walking with fierce determination, his head down, striding fast, swinging his cane, Grange walked straight past Hargood, moving in the opposite direction. Their courses took them several paces further before Hargood called out:

"Silas!"

Grange turned round, drawn out of his thoughts.

"My dear fellow," Hargood said, "you stared straight through me."

Grange held out a hand, which Hargood proceeded to shake with vigorous abandon.

"Hargood, I apologize most humbly for not seeing you."

"I'll not ask you what you were thinking about. Now, listen . . ." Hargood was conspiratorial. "I was out the other day riding in one of my fields when by good luck or accident I saw, in a piece of adjoining woodland which by chance I happen to own"—Hargood glanced to left and right briefly, as if to enhance the dramatic nature of his revelation—"a magnificent pair of antlers. Some damned fine stag had escaped from Lord Alcombe's estate and wandered onto my property. By rights of owning the land on which it stood, I claim precedence. I went back home, got my flintlock, crept up on the beast and . . . well, it's hung and ready for eating."

Grange smiled, despite himself, at the thought of Hargood's genial roguery. If he was not firing buckshot at the rear of Salt Officers, he was cannoning deer.

"Hargood, you are incorrigible."

"Now, Silas, all I need is someone to help me dispose of the evidence of this most disgraceful affair. You seem sufficiently wicked to me to be my accomplice. What about dinner tonight, old fellow? Do you have the stomach, or will you disappoint me?"

"I have both the stomach and the wickedness. I accept without a moment's hesitation."

Hargood punched him affectionately on the shoulder.

"Good man. Let me clear some paperwork. If you arrive at seven thirty, we can set about the dastardly deed."

"At seven thirty."

They parted and Grange walked on. But the interlude proved little more than a respite from his preoccupations. A few moments later, his thoughts once more turned to Mrs. Quill and Jane, and his mind drifted downward through the surface of his reverie into a more serious concentration.

· · ·

At the head of the table, Hargood carved large, thick slices of venison. Seated at Hargood's right hand, like the Prodigal Son, Grange watched the knife probe and part the flesh. Hargood passed a huge plate to Grange, then lavishly filled his own.

"Don't stand on ceremony, my dear fellow. Start in."

While Grange began to eat as bidden, Hargood piled extra slices on his own plate. Dark trains of blood ran to the edges of the carving dish.

"By God, this is good meat."

When he had finished carving, Hargood refilled his own and Grange's glass with red wine. He raised his glass in a toast.

"To crime."

Grange smiled.

"To crime."

Hargood began to devour his meat with gusto. Grange could hear his incisors slicing the meat, the hiss of moisture beneath his tongue. Out of the side of his mouth, Hargood said:

"You looked very concentrated today, Silas."

"Oh?" Grange asked.

"Yes, and don't play the innocent."

Hargood ate animatedly, drank, ate again: "A penny for your thoughts."

"Then or now?"

"Both."

Grange paused to clear his thoughts before addressing himself once again to the subject. Hargood masticated a piece of meat, swallowed, swooped for the next forkful.

"Is it Mrs. Quill?" Hargood asked.

Unused to this level of perception on the part of his host, Grange was taken by surprise. At the same time, apparently unaware of his penetrating shot, Hargood continued to eat noisily. He raised his glass.

"Here's to women and good red meat."

They raised their glasses and toasted.

"If you must know, Hargood," Grange said, "I do think of her."

Hargood, faithful to the rhythm of his eating, took his time: "Remarkable woman, as I've said. Handsome, too."

Grange paused. Hargood ate noisily.

"Extracting answers from you, my dear Silas, is like extracting teeth."

"What would you like to know?"

Hargood was too busy devouring a heavy flange of thigh meat to answer immediately. He first shifted the meat from his incisors to his molars.

"What would you like to tell me?"

There was another silence while Hargood guzzled enthusiastically.

"Another helping? No? Hope you don't mind if I help myself." Hargood assisted himself liberally. "Imagine your thoughts are like this meat, dear fellow. Let them fall away, slice by slice."

"So that you may consume them?"

"It depends if there's anything to consume," Hargood said good-naturedly. "It's for your own good."

Hargood paused to pull a thin line of gristle from his teeth with his thick fingers, and with a grunt lay the offending strand at the side of his plate. He watched Grange eat, pointing briefly with his knife at Grange's somewhat surgical use of knife and fork.

"Damn me, Silas, you think too much. You slice your meat so awful fine."

"Hargood, I know you mean well. It's just that there are certain subjects . . ."

"Certain subjects? I see. If you will not talk, sir, then I will do so on your behalf. I will tell you what I know of Mrs. Quill. Or will you forbid me from even mentioning her?"

"You are at liberty to talk as you see fit."

"Good," Hargood said. "Good enough." While he paused, he drank from the glass. "Mrs. Quill is a woman of high repute. I like her. But there are certain things I shall admit I do not fully understand."

"For example."

"For example, she has been here three years only. Before that, she came from London. I never met her husband."

"And what is so very strange about that?"

"Nothing, nothing." Hargood moved his tongue around in his mouth, searching for a stray piece of meat. "She has never told me precisely what her husband did. I grant you that's not strange in itself. But it's my experience that widows of long marriages continue to talk about their husbands—most of them."

"You think there was a . . . tragedy?"

"A tragedy?" Hargood shrugged. "Perhaps." He returned to his eating. In due course he finished his mouthful, pushed his plate aside.

"Most excellent meat . . . You know, Silas, what gives me special satisfaction is that Lord Alcombe, who in the past has enjoyed the inestimable benefits of my service as physician, conveniently decided to overlook my last bill. Oh, I'll get it back when he next needs me, but all the same, it's satisfying to receive compensation." Hargood belched. "Forgive them, Father." He raised his glass. "Here's to neighboring estates, tight-fisted noblemen, and natural justice."

Grange raised his glass.

"Natural justice."

Hargood leaned back, surveying the table with satisfaction. The conversation had become disjointed, and several seconds now passed without further comment. Hargood eased his belt and placed a satisfied hand on his stomach. Grange continued to pick at his meat.

"You mentioned a tragedy?" Grange asked.

"Tragedy? Not exactly. To be correct, it was you who mentioned a possible tragedy. Myself, I'm not so sure."

"Hargood, you say that I am tight with my answers."

"Yes, I do, don't I?" Hargood agreed. "What I have to offer on the subject of tragedy is merely a feeling—an intuition, if you like. In my dealings with widows, they usually carry the mark of their husbands. It is nearly always very clear. They keep mementos, they refer to them almost without thinking. If they are faced with a financial transaction, or a problem in the maintenance of the house, they invoke their husbands' names. It is automatic, like invoking our Lord in times of distress. Mrs. Quill does not. Mrs. Quill," Hargood added, "is unmarked."

"Unmarked?"

"In fact, I sometimes rather wonder whether she ever had a husband."

Too many thoughts moved inside Grange's head to be expressed.

"She has deceived you about her husband?"

"Good heavens, no, my dear fellow. Crude though I may be, I won't dream of saying she is lying. She has been perfectly direct with me, and to all others I know. More than direct. I would say she is marked by a particular honesty. Unlike Lord Alcombe, she pays my bills. Her marriage must have been unusual, though, one of those things that simply pass. I am merely saying that she is curiously unmarked by widowhood."

Hargood paused.

"Is that all?" Grange felt, despite these doubts, a strange sense of relief.

Hargood moved his head from side to side slowly, as though considering. "Yes . . . More wine?"

"Thank you."

"Good man." Hargood reached toward Grange's glass with the bottle.

"And what about you, Hargood?" Grange asked divertingly. "You take such a kind interest in my affairs. How are yours?"

"My mistress serves me well. I shall be visiting her in London again the week after next, by the way. Strangely enough, knowing our esteemed widow Mrs. Quill hails from London,

I asked my young lady whether she had heard of her or her late husband in society. She said her name rang a bell, but she did not know which bell, or why it rang."

"You are incorrigible. If I am not certain, you will have a full investigation next."

Hargood reached toward the decanter. The liquid in the low candlelight glowed dark, blood red.

"Then, of course," Hargood said, "there are her teeth."

Grange laughed. "Hargood, I do believe that you take the comparison between women and horses too far."

Hargood allowed a half smile to pass across his features.

"Teeth, my dear fellow, are very interesting, particularly in London."

Hargood raised the decanter from the table toward Grange, an interrogative gesture. Grange shook his head. Hargood filled his own glass and replaced the top of the decanter. Now he raised his glass and sniffed the liquid in the French style, lost in his own thoughts.

"I suppose I had better humor you," Grange conceded, "and enquire what you imply."

Hargood was content to take his time.

"To those of us who look for willing fillies, teeth are sometimes an interesting clue to the background of the subject. In London particularly, for the past fifty years or more, there has been a great fashion for sweetness amongst the wealthier classes. They take sugar in their tea, they add it to their drinks, they make their confections sickly sweet. Indeed, they have taken to making a variety of confections which seem nothing but sugar and air. Hardly a meal goes by without some sweet at the end of it. There are certain shops and bakeries that cater almost exclusively to these tastes. It is particularly the case amongst women, who take constant sweet beverages. I do not pretend to know the mechanism, but the consequences of this addiction to sweetness have now perhaps become more obvious. The fact is, the teeth of the women of the fashionable classes are half decayed away."

Hargood paused. "You may take my word for it, sir. In our capital, bad teeth have become a sign of good breeding. The lower orders, who until now could not afford sugar, are largely exempt. They may suffer from their nutrition, from various diseases, but if one looks into the mouth of a young scullery maid, one sees the healthy dentition of an animal."

Hargood paused to raise his glass for viewing and slowly rotated it, watching the deep red lights. "I should say that Mrs. Quill's teeth belong in the second category."

"And what, then, do you deduce?" Grange asked.

"I deduce, my friend, that she either has most extreme fine natural teeth, that she has an aversion to sweetness, or that, in her origins, she does not come from the fashionable classes."

In the silence the thirty or so candles above the table puffed and billowed. Outside, a flurry of wind hit the windowpanes. Breaths of cool air slid under the doors.

"Let us suppose, then, that her rise in society is recent," Grange asked. "What of it?"

"Always her defender, Silas," Hargood said with a smile. "I may choose to deduce very little, except that Mrs. Quill is like one of those kaleidoscopes that do amuse children at fairs. One turn, and another brilliant scene unfolds. Almost every aspect of her which I care to consider leaves me uncomfortably unsure of my assumptions. As a doctor, I am concerned with diagnosis. If Mrs. Quill were a condition, rather than a person, I would grant you that I am not in full appreciation of the facts."

"Those features which make you uncomfortable," Grange persisted, "I would merely call exceptional."

"Ah yes, exceptional," Hargood mused. "I'll grant you exceptionality."

Later that evening, Dr. Grange said: "Dr. Craig put teeth from a dead man into different solutions, which he labeled and observed from day to day, and found that which decayed the most was Indian sugar, beet was second, honey the third in order of guilt. Or so I was taught in Edinburgh."

"Edinburgh be damned." Hargood appeared concerned that his line of reasoning was about to be abducted by Grange's more recent knowledge. "It is a mere hypothesis, and my argument depends on it merely in a technical sense, for now we may leave it aside and concentrate upon the fact. I repeat, the teeth of the women of fashion are rotted away, whether the cause be Indian cane or beet sugar or honey or some other cause. That, sir, is what leads me to my point."

"What point is that?" Grange asked, deliberately obtuse.

"I have seen her smile. She does not smile often, and that is why I remark upon it. For when she smiles, I see the most perfectly formed white teeth I have ever seen."

"Yet I merely rejoice in her smile, and you would criticize me for that?"

"She has taken you under her wing, she has confided in you in some sense which I do not understand, and she has conquered you. I am in favor of my colleagues being conquered by women, not least by one as fine as that. I am particularly in favor of you being conquered by a woman. Yet she leaves me uneasy."

"Is it not the case that all fine and fearful things leave one uneasy? That is part of their attraction."

"Will you laugh at me?" Hargood asked. "Do, sir, pray, and perhaps I will tell when you laugh again what it is that concerns me."

Hargood raised the decanter, though Grange sensed a slowing in his manner. He filled their glasses:

"Silas, I am not often serious. I am not, like you, a rationalist. I am a man of feeling—some would say vulgar feeling. I will say no more on this matter, except to ask you to be careful. You are dealing with a formidable woman, whose past is mysterious. That is my last word."

Grange raised his glass.

"I'll drink to that."

Hargood smiled. They drank. Hargood amiably watched as Grange continued to pick at the meat on his dish.

"Put your meat aside, dear fellow. You've done enough. I'll have it cold tomorrow. The prospect of eating Lord Alcombe's prized stag means that I shall consume the entire animal myself if necessary, hot, warm, or cold as the grave."

27

*I*t was when he faced toward the marshes, turning out of the Oxey wood like a dark stair, that a figure rode out of the darkness, a bull of a man, carrying a sack over one shoulder. The other arm was free, a scarecrow's arm, flapping. Grange experienced a moment of fear, but the sudden loss of privacy was, if anything, a deeper embarrassment. He found it hard not to feel a flare of resentment, and put aside thoughts that he had met a brigand out on the foreshore. He did not even wish to look out of his own thoughts into the man's face, and sensed a similar reticence on the part of the other. So they passed at perhaps five feet distance, driving past one another like animals in their individual trails.

Only when they were abreast and Grange observed starfall on the other's profile, did he recognize the features. "Swann," he called out involuntarily. The figure halted and swung, turning his heavy, white face toward the white light of the shore, enough to verify Grange's observation. At the same time as he recognized his former patient, he observed the other's surprise. Grange, his face in shadow by virtue of facing the dark wood, suspected that as author of the cry, he must be virtually unrecognizable.

Yet somehow Swann had identified his voice, and an expression like a cautious grin spread across the seaman's face. Sudden curiosity stung Grange. Swann seemed hale, even in this light, after hardly more than three weeks since Grange peremptorily had sawed off his arm. There was about Swann's strong torso, his carriage, a shining power—though he seemed, even in darkness, light on one side.

"How are you?" Grange asked. Given the drastic nature of the medicine, his question sounded tentative. Swann paused a few seconds, considering his reply.

"Seldom felt better."

Was it bravado? Grange asked himself. Was such a rapid recovery possible? Yet when challenged, there was something graceful in the way that Swann swung, moving perfectly balanced on his feet with what seemed the added burden of a heavy shoulder bag. With the loss of an arm on one side, surely it would take months to reestablish the natural fluidities of bodily grace, to learn to feel comfortable in this redistribution of weights? Swann saw or sensed Grange's eyes move toward his shoulder, where the dark load was like a hump.

"Driftwood and chippings," Swann confirmed. "Waterlogged, but I'll spread them in the sun; they'll be good for firewood by the end of the week." At the same time, noting Grange's eyes on his empty sleeve, Swann said, "I fit my clothes well, sir, like you said."

"So I observe."

A lapse occurred, and for several moments silence moved palpably between them. Then Swann was agitated, nodding, indicating with his head something behind Grange. Over the Solent, where the water glimmered in the Hurst narrows, a powerful black cloud was beginning to obscure the light. Behind or beneath it a sea breeze was rising, as cold as a shadow. "A gale's coming," Swann said.

"You will know about gales," Grange replied, following the niceties of convention. "Our provision of weather here is often strange, is it not?"

"Indeed, sir."

"One may have hail at Lepe, and pure sunshine at Buckland."

"That's as may be," Swann said approvingly, following the agreed line of discourse. "But there is a pattern in between. Storm clouds come in, slide west of Pennington, toward Sway, and if they are unloading lightning, sir, they always go up the valley . . ."

"Sway Valley?"

". . . And drop a shaft or two on Colonel Buller's house. I've seen one cloud black as night, spitting forked fire like a galleon."

Grange smiled, the dark wind at his neck.

"Colonel Buller?"

"He's had three direct strikes in seven years. In a storm all the scullery maids whimper, sir. The dogs hide under the tables. He and his wife make themselves ready with buckets of water to damp a fire, as if they are about to be invaded by the French, or even worse, the Dutch."

"He lives in fear, then?"

"One bolt came down the chimney; fused a set of knives in his kitchen into a single clump, like a twist of snakes. A girl that used to work there saw a ball of lightning the size of a cat move slowly across the landing. Pinned to the wall, she was. Left to right, she said it moved; calm as a priest."

"You have a good ear for description," Grange said.

Swann nodded at the cloud building behind Grange.

"Land storms aren't much, though." Swann was dismissive. "Nothing like an electric storm at sea. That's danger, sir. You're as exposed as a rat on a bowling lawn. There isn't a tree or a tussock to hide behind."

"You've seen some yourself," Grange suggested.

"Certainly, sir. The worst off the French coast. Down close by St. Malo. You know the place?"

"No," Grange replied, "but please continue."

"You have time?" Swann seemed suddenly guilty at his talk.

"I have time. Such phenomena interest me. An electric storm, you said."

Swann seemed to hesitate still out of something like shyness, then continued.

"It came over calm suddenly, the sky turning green and gold and black, and thunder you could hear for three hours. Sheet lightning on the horizon to the west. As it bore closer, St. Bartholomew's fire in the rigging, no one able to look one another in the eye for fear. Not a breath of air, terrible; you can smell your own insides."

"You could not sail?"

"Not a stitch of wind. You do what you can for taking your mind off it. If you lay chain from the mast and hang it over the side so that it lies in the water, it is said to ward off the electrics. Then the lightning gets closer and you can see it striking down into the water, raising steam. It is terrible. And nothing to do but wait. In a battle you can fire back."

"Was your ship hit?" Grange tried to hide the note of hope in his voice.

"The storm went right over, striking the water all around us. Over and through, leaving us untouched. When we thought we could breathe at last, it struck a blow from behind. On the mizzen. A terrible roar, and then white fire in the aft wheelhouse creeping over the top and starting to climb the lower mizzen cordage like sparks. We put it out with seawater easy enough, helped by a heavy shower of rain. But for several days after, your nerve is gone. You feel like a barrel, empty on the inside. You sense you've been selected."

Reluctantly breaking off, sensing perhaps that to ask for more was to exceed the finely balanced relations of courtesy between their different stations of life, Grange asked: "And your family is well?"

So they changed the subject from this to that, standing on a barren footpath, a storm rising behind. Grange heard the news of Swann's family, his common-law wife and several daughters, then bid farewell and took his leave. Yet as he strolled on, striking forward, his mind was full of the images of lightning and fire. Despite these thoughts, a strange sense of relief entered his mind. The talk with Swann had eased some nagging pain in his soul. Now that he had witnessed his patient to all intents and purposes healthy without his left appendage, Grange began to hope, even to believe, that he would have no further dreams of Swann's lopped arm hitting the dish.

But quietude in one compartment of the mind often leads merely to focusing on the restlessness of another. While they had been talking, the night had darkened further. Now as he set his course, a new coldness began to rise out of the earth. Grange returned toward the house, walking along quiet ditches in whose scattered surface water were reflected the shining loam, silent grass stems, the low mass of Hurst Castle, and the last of the disappearing stars.

28

The following Saturday, shortly before dawn, he was woken by Mrs. Thompson standing above his bed in her long night-gown, a coat thrown over her shoulders. It had been a cold night for summer, and he had turned away and lain on his side, his legs drawn up, the better to preserve warmth. She held a candle in one hand while she shook his shoulder with the other. He groaned, opened his eyes, turned over, and saw her own gaze withdraw from his as she whispered, "You asked to be woken early, sir. Five thirty."

"Thank you, Mrs. Thompson."

She nodded and drifted through the door.

The passengers for the early coaches congregated at the Hope and Anchor Inn. Sleepy, dazed by their own movement, they sat without speaking in the smoke-stained waiting room. Several transports left Lymington early for other destinations. On weekdays, the Telegraph stagecoach departed every morning at the unconscionable hour of 5:00 A.M. so that it might arrive in Southampton by 7:30. From the Nag's Head another coach, the Independent, left at the same time also for Southampton. To Grange, this was the early morning sound, of horses' hooves against cobbles, the scream of the brakes, and the grinding of stones beneath metal as the wheels slewed around the corner into the open street. It was the commotion of the departing coaches, rather than Mrs. Thompson, which usually woke him. Yet now that he was up, he enjoyed the small ceremony of shaving; resolving not to light a candle, he shaved himself in darkness largely by feel, running the strop across his cheeks, chin, and neck until the skin was tolerably smooth. He toweled his face dry and, while the slowly increasing light resolved the room into its calm angularities, he began to dress.

Downstairs, Mrs. Thompson had left cold ham and cheese on the table, and a cup and pitcher of water. By now it was light enough to see. Resolving to put something in his stomach against the journey, he cut himself several slices of ham and swilled it down with cold, fresh water. Whatever his preoccupations, the prospect of travel was always bracing to him, and he left the house carrying his valise a few minutes later in reasonable spirits, swinging the door to softly in case Mrs. Thompson had returned to sleep.

His own transport, the coach to Salisbury, was a little later; six fifteen, a heavier, slower vehicle than the Southampton Telegraph, with eight horses. The coachman, a Brockenhurst man by the name of Chalder, stood by as the passengers mounted the steps, and helped the ladies stow their baggage. When the horses strained forward, the coachman eased the brake and they accelerated slowly. In motion, the coach reminded Grange of one of those slow river barges that drifts forward under its own momentum. Once started, it maintained a slow but even speed. After leaving the High Street, it swung almost due north through the forest, following a meandering track through Burley, aiming to arrive in Salisbury by early afternoon.

Glass having been substituted for the leather blinds, the light rendered it more difficult to sleep. But if he placed his hat over his face and closed his eyes, the noise of the wheels on the gravel roads would soon settle him, sending him, if not directly to sleep, then to some tolerable halfway stage of rest or intermittent dreaming. The transport swayed like a ship, which he liked, though generally speaking the introduction of suspension to coaches had been a mixed blessing. The coach's swaying brought on a growing sickness in some, a terrible *mal-de-mer*. There was a sickly residual smell that vinegar and scrubbing had not entirely dispelled.

Yet Grange loved these journeys. On the heavy, swaying, coach he usually found a corner seat so that, if he was not dozing, he could stare out over the gently rolling landscape and heaths of the New Forest. Occasionally the coach drew up and halted to pay tolls at the various tollgates on their path. But its progress was steady. Sometimes the other passengers struck up a conversation. He was not inclined to be sociable, but became an island to himself, lost in his own thoughts.

At Downton village green in early afternoon sunlight he alighted, carrying his valise in one hand, and gained brief directions from the driver concerning his destination. The weather being clear, and with nothing more than a valise for luggage, rather than hire a horse or even a brougham from the village ostlery, he decided to walk the two miles along Eastern

Road to the gates of Mrs. Pugh's house. There was little traffic of any description. The road, he found, was not much more than a cart track. Solitary blackbirds scattered from it as he walked. Above him rooks moved in small flocks, so high they could hardly be seen.

In due course he turned off the track and walked down a huge ride of trees toward the main house, hidden by a line of beeches. It was a sunny afternoon. As he continued down the ride, a disembodied noise approached, a squeaking, restless sound, running parallel with him behind a line of yew hedges. The sound converged with him at an intersection of paths, and an elderly, white-haired gardener emerged and passed him pushing a wheelbarrow.

"Good-day, sir."

Grange nodded in acknowledgment.

The ride took a turn at its end, so that suddenly and unexpectedly the great house and its shadows towered over him. He looked upward at its many windows, set between stone mullions. The house had an unsettling calm, perhaps augmented by its remoteness from other habitations. He was approaching the main entrance now, walking up the great flagstone staircase. Putting down his valise, he briefly adjusted his coat and knocked on the massive front door. He heard footsteps echoing in the interior and not long afterward the heavy door was opened with a formal discharge of bolts. A tall butler appeared, executing a brisk, formal inclination of the head. "Harrison, sir."

"Good afternoon. Dr. Grange."

"Madam is expecting you. May I take your luggage?"

Harrison, the valise innocuous in his right hand, led him through a huge hall, through its empty spaces, paintings and stuffed animal-heads above him, the shine of beeswax on dark furniture, a polished silence.

Harrison, meanwhile, maintained a polite and running discourse. "Madam has tea in her private garden at this time, sir. She requested me expressly to escort you there. She permits no one else in the garden excepting guests." Opening the door, he inclined his head as Grange passed through:

"Madam is around that corner. I'll take your luggage to your room, sir."

"Thank you."

Harrison's tepid smile floated backward in the gloom. The door closed behind Grange, and for a moment he allowed his eyes to adjust to the outside brilliance. So unexpected was the garden after the cool interior of the house, it was as if he had traveled here through a Minotaur's tunnel. He glanced around at the scene, with its pleasant flower beds and shrubs, its scents and birdsong, and somewhere the sound of running water. His eyes having adjusted to the outside brightness, he began to walk in the direction Harrison had indicated, turning a corner of yew hedges, which threw open before his eyes a fresh scene.

A stone cupid stood beside a fountain, on its face an expression of permanent, cheerful surprise. One hand with its small fingers held a beaker, out of which water gushed into a fish pond. To its right was a small enclosure of hedges. At the furthest corner Mrs. Pugh was seated in a cane chair, beneath a parasol, dressed in a simple white silk gown which had the effect of showing off her figure. A tea tray was on the table. She appeared engrossed in a book that lay open on the table before her.

As he started toward her, walking briskly, she seemed to recede, as if the garden were slowing time. Then, almost as suddenly, he was beside her. So taken with her reading did she seem that he was almost directly facing her before she recognized his presence. She put down her book and stood up.

"My dear Dr. Grange. It is good to see you."

"Good-day, madam."

Observing the expression on his face, her pleasure at seeing him was plain. Indicating the other cane chair, she said, "Please sit down."

Seated once again, she glanced down at the dust on his boots, and asked with some consternation: "You have walked?"

"A mile or two, madam. I came by stage to the village and walked from there."

"My dear sir, I could have arranged for you to be collected by carriage from the village."

"I enjoy walking, I do assure you, madam. I walk whenever I am able."

She appeared to accept his explanation, though somewhat reluctantly. Now, pausing delicately, her hand on the teapot, she asked as if struck by thought:

"You have eaten?"

"An excellent breakfast, madam. I do not eat much at midday."

"Are you certain? I believe I should call Harrison, and ask him to bring a plate . . ."

"I am certain, though your offer is kind."

"Tea, then?"

"Thank you. If you will forgive my innocent enthusiasm, madam, you inhabit a beautiful garden."

"I thank you. It is my refuge." She handed him a cup, and began to pour her own. "We are not overlooked at all. It affords me perfect privacy."

Grange stared around him at the flowers, the shrubs, the trimmed hedges. Birds sang and insects chirped in the background, though what he began to witness now, in this garden of sunlight, was not sound but smell, the hidden current of flowers. Against which the scent of the tea was sharp, delicious. Engrossed, the movement of his attention drifted from the garden to her amiable conversation. She lowered her hand in passing to rearrange the soft silk of her dress.

"My father used to have such a garden," Mrs. Pugh said. "I played in it when a child. It was my own small world, in which I could do much as I liked."

"It is charming, madam."

"That childhood garden I have tried to re-create. But it is as if I pursued a dream. I remember that a pond lay on the other side of a maze, yet at the same time I imagined I could view the pond as if the maze were not there. I have followed these fancies as best I am able, though stitching together dream and recollection is a strange kind of knitting."

"It must be, yet you have succeeded."

"If that garden ever existed, to a certain degree I believe

I have succeeded in achieving its echo. When you have finished your tea, perhaps you will permit me to show you its extent."

"I should be honored." He glanced around, attempting to gauge its extremity. Certain recesses and walls were in deep shadow, so that he could not observe their entirety. Amongst occasional distracting bees and summer sun, he imagined it at nightfall, its shapes and curves held in long shadows.

"To focus the sense of smell," Mrs. Pugh remarked, "one must close the eyes."

If he did so, the formless shape of the garden emerged in his mind, like an imaginative presence. As he opened his eyes again, she observed him, smiling at his inhibition. Out of displacement he drank his tea.

In the distance thunder rang. It was like the faint echo of cutlery. Mrs. Pugh watched the direction of his eyes to the clouds that grew dark in the west: "Rain?"

"Later, I think."

Seeds floated down to the stone borders. He imagined them yellow like sunlight.

"More tea, sir?"

"No, thank you."

Perhaps the clouds had reminded Mrs. Pugh of time, for now that he had finished his tea, she stood up and took him by the hand. He followed her without resistance. "This is a replica of the pool around which I played." She drew him along after her. "These are the shrubs between which I would hide, sir, from fears and fancies." Drawing him through a maze of yew hedges, her fingers curled and uncurled around his, pressing them against the firm, curved base of her thumb. Playfully, he protested: "Madam, I fear I am already lost."

"We are all lost in life, sir."

Now he seemed part of her forward motion, a moon following a planet. Herb beds of chervil, marjoram, basil, sorrel. Her forward motion imparted a breeze, so that her silk dress floated out behind her. Rows of bulbs in shallow drills, in one place a spade beside newly turned earth, work interrupted. It occurred to him that there must be a gardener in this her private paradise, like an animal unseen.

Mrs. Pugh turned to face him. She appeared flushed with excitement.

"Close your eyes, sir. This garden is in the mind. I will turn you round three times. Then you must find me."

His mild objections were nothing more than air. He closed his eyes and she spun him three times. When he opened them, she had disappeared entirely. Searching for signs of her, he made a complete circle. The garden appeared empty, sightless.

"Madam?" Grange asked.

He was amused at first. He looked for her behind a yew hedge, investigated the space behind some shrubs, then he searched along a wall lined with fruit trees. After several such vain attempts, however, he began to be disconcerted.

"Madam?"

In one corner there was a herb garden, a complex Elizabethan knot, with pathways of brick and filled with herbs: parsley, thyme, mint, chervil, dill. The whiteness of scattered marguerites, like ghosts. Crossing the herb garden, he perceived a gap in the hedge on the other side, toward what appeared to be an arbor. But when he reached it, and passed through an arch of hedges, it was merely the gateway to other arbors.

Hesitantly at first, then with greater speed, as if now that he was lost he might proceed with a kind of abandon, Grange began to walk down a long hedge into which were set other arbors, in what seemed to him an infinite regress. In several of the arbors were statues, mostly of human forms. In one was a satyr or Pan, staring forward as if into a perspective which only he could see. Yet as Grange's own breath slid fresh through him, his mind somewhat shocked at the arousal of the satyr's private parts, he became aware of the strange layout of the garden, and its relation to the mind. But his search had gained some momentum and seemed to drive itself, for he continued to half walk and half run down the corridor. In another arbor was a statue of a naked nymph fleeing, looking backward over her shoulder.

Now, as he traveled, fresh perspectives opened, though none contained Mrs. Pugh. It was as if the garden itself had become a maze, or region of the mind, and only displayed what it was predisposed to show. Further down the corridor of hedges, in a yet further arbor, a satyr had caught up with a nymph, who bent forward lasciviously while he seized her from the rear.

"Silas?"

In the spinning world, Mrs. Pugh peered at him over her shoulder, bending forward, her skirts raised high to expose her thighs.

"Come, sir, it is time to follow nature."

Now it was Grange whose senses swam alarmed, who heard the sounds of a human couple's enjoyment as if at a distance. He felt she welcomed all of his human qualities in this still garden, raucous with silence. Between her deeper sighs, Mrs. Pugh said:

"You will stay overnight, I trust, sir."

29

Afterwards, from what seemed a further perspective of time, he sat in the paneled study, reading a book while his hostess dressed for dinner. It had rained upon them. With strict instructions not to seek them, Harrison had assumed they had taken shelter in the garden beneath one of the trees or overhanging ledges. When they emerged into the house, dripping from their sojourn, at a whispered word from Mrs.

Pugh, Harrison had led Grange up the stairs to his bedroom and supplied a beaker of hot water and a washbasin. Having seen to her guest's requirements, Mrs. Pugh herself departed to her bedroom to wash and change.

While Grange was washing, Harrison discreetly removed his clothes and carried them downstairs to dry before the fire in the kitchen. Having washed himself, Grange changed into his more formal attire for dinner.

In the study it was gloomy, the sky itself still being overcast, and the contents difficult to perceive. On one side of the rampart of the desk stood a bright brass lamp in the shape of a snake. In place of a shade it had been fitted with a small glass luster. As a sort of courtesy, an embarrassment almost, induced by the gloomy weather, Harrison had lit the wick, and by its illumination Grange could read. Though he attempted to concentrate his mind upon the vellum pages, his thoughts seemed dispersed. His mind could not help but return to what had taken place. For in spite of his attempt at concentration, the images of desire rose through the page and the letters themselves, like light floating upward through water. He was thus engaged, his mind not so much reflective as refractive, when Mrs. Pugh knocked on the door and entered. Grange observed, outside the lake of light spread by the lamp, her shrewd and humorous face glide toward him.

"You are ready for supper, sir?"

He stood up and faced her, and for a moment it seemed that they both smiled at the expression that each saw there—in her case, the smile of a hostess who believes she has entertained more than expected; in his own, the disconcerted but grateful glance of a surprised guest.

"Harrison has taken your clothes to dry?"

"Yes, madam."

The details of clothes as a rule did not concern him; in fact, he deliberately shut them from his mind as something largely without bearing on his own concerns. Yet now he seemed attuned to surfaces of things. She moved toward the door, and he observed a high-waisted silk dress, in classic mode, with a short overgarment against the chill that had arisen with the evening. Her hair was tied elegantly in what was fashionably called a Clytie knot, high at the back of her head. She hesitated in the doorway and waited for him to come alongside her, then took his arm and walked by his side into the dining room.

The ubiquitous Harrison had seen to it that a great fire blazed in there, sending flames like sharp spears upward.

Mrs. Pugh sat decorously at the head of the table, Grange on her right. There were no other guests. Harrison served turtle soup from a silver tureen, and in a silence that was punctuated sometimes by sharp cracks from the fire, Mrs. Pugh waited until Harrison had gone before she smiled at Grange.

"My dear sir, I think it is time we knew each other by our Christian names. I hope I may call you Silas. My Christian name is Arabella, as you know, but my friends—and I trust that you shall allow me to count you among them—call me Bella."

"Thank you."

Mrs. Pugh lowered her voice:

"For appearances sake, I have given you one of the further bedrooms. I shall pass by this evening, if you wish."

"That is kind of you, and welcome."

Beneath the table, as if to emphasize her thoughts, she placed a calm and perhaps possessive hand on his leg.

"Tomorrow, I am afraid, I shall not see you. I shall go to Confession, for my sins. Are you one of the flock, Silas?"

"No. I am not religious."

She paused to consider him.

"That is why, perhaps, you are forced to struggle with your conscience. Speaking for myself, I require absolution. I took to the Roman Church after my husband died. I find faith is such a consolation."

"I am pleased that you find it so."

"Let us retire early, sir. I will join you. But I must leave your room before twelve. Sunday is a sacred day."

"I shall respect your wishes, you may be sure. Each thing in its place."

"Exactly so. In church, I prefer to meet a priest; in bed, I am prepared to meet an unbeliever."

Shortly afterward, for discretion's sake, she removed her hand when Harrison made his appearance and proceeded to gather their dishes. After he left, she smiled again.

"I like you well, Silas." She lowered her voice. "You are a combination of gentleman and faun."

"You praise me too much."

They began to talk, though afterward Grange could not recall the details of their discussion. It seemed to expand by itself, without volition. He remembered simply an atmosphere of lightheartedness, and the inconsequentiality of the subjects that occupied his attention was perhaps part of the charm of the evening. The preponderance of well-being, the cheerful and brisk fire that was regularly sustained by Harrison, and the excellent food and wine, seemed to lull that sense of watchfulness which formed his usual isolation. When they retired to their respective bedrooms, he waited for her to join him.

Mrs. Pugh said, "Do not put out the candle, my sweet."

On the side table the little light flickered. In its shadows Grange caught glimpses of flesh. Mrs. Pugh raised her shift; a fine leg, an arc of stomach, at the base of the stomach a V of pubic hair.

"Candles remind me of church, and of music," Mrs. Pugh said. Her shift came off her and rose toward the ceiling like a flame. Naked, she had that fullness which he considered attractive. Her lips touched his. She raised his hands to her breasts.

Kneeling between his knees, he could not see her face at all, just the curve of her dark hair where the light bounced as her head moved gently. All he could know of her was a voice, sometimes a gasp of pleasure.

"Speak of music," Mrs. Pugh suggested, "of church music. Tell me what you like."

There was darkness again and he yearned for light, the thin beam from her helmet of hair, the delicate line of her ribs, the base of her spine, the shadow of her rear.

"Madam, I like above all Thomas Tallis's *Service in the Dorian Mode*, consisting of the *Venite*, *Te Deum*, *Benedictus*, *Kyrie*, *Nicene Creed*, *Sanctus*, *Gloria in Excelsis*, *Magnificat*, and *Nunc Dimittis*, for four voices, together with the *Preces*, *Responses*, *Paternoster*, and *Litany*, for five."

Crouched there, she was silent and contained.

"All were published in the Reverend John Barnard's *First Book of Selected Church Music*. In Boyce's *Cathedral Music*, neither the *Paternoster* nor the *Venite* was included. Omission of the beautiful *Venite* is hard to account for. In my own Boyce's version, I have enclosed a pamphlet with a *Venite*. The forty-part motet *Spem in alium* is a *tour de force*."

The sap rising, he looked along the faint, luminous curve of her vertebrae. She was moving her hips back and forth slowly. Now she was humming something, for he could feel the vibrations through her lips and tongue, as if it might be sacred music. It was shocking and voluptuous. He was determined to maintain the flow of discourse.

"In his *Miserere Nostri*," Grange continued, "the intricacy of the contrapuntal devices seems little short of miraculous."

Miraculous, too, was the flow of feeling toward the tip, as if his whole universe was there. In London, the whores, particularly those of French and Italian origin, would do this as a special favor. But here, in this atmosphere of respectability, it took on its own ambience. He gasped and shuddered, then recovered sufficiently to continue.

"Of course, it is sometimes difficult to distinguish between the work of Tallis and his pupil and collaborator, Byrd. In Tallis's later life, certain works are explicitly acknowledged to Byrd. For example, *Cantiones quae ab argumento Sacrae Vocantur, quinque et sex partium* consists of sixteen motets by Tallis and eighteen by Byrd."

The candle remained on the floor where she had placed it, sending out a quiet, softly pulsing light. He felt his being slide under the shadowy pleasures of her hands and mouth.

"The music is perhaps too sensuous for the Protestant faith," Grange added. "I am not the only one in believing so. Though both Tallis and Byrd conformed outwardly to the new religion, they remained Catholics at heart."

Yet he was never so aware of light, or its absence. A single flame was a tiny illumination. Even a huge chandelier, lowered so that the candles might be lit at ground level and then hoisted toward the ceiling, would give only a faint *luminus* to a large room. The night was black in the corners. It created an atmosphere half of waking, half dream. Dark furniture took on an angular solidity. White flesh glowed concupiscent. Now she rose toward him, her heavy auburn hair. He kissed her cheek, her mouth, as she pushed him gently backward. Out of the darkness, as out of an ocean, emerged shoulder, breast, the darker shadow of armpit or pudendum. He and Mrs. Pugh were lovers in their strange, dark sea.

When they were finished, she turned away not to sleep, but to rise from the bed so that she might adhere to her own curfew of departing before midnight. She drew her shift over her, gave what seemed a half sigh of pleasure or regret, and left. Something inexplicable lay itching in his memory, causing him to lie awake.

What did he feel? Not self-disgust, certainly. The experience had been pleasurable. He was under the sway of a genuine liking for Mrs. Pugh. There was something strikingly honest and direct about her, something rational. Was it disappointment that afflicted him now? A sense of standing suspended, of something unfulfilled? The great rakes, he suspected, experienced this emotional disappointment as no more than an astringent. It might be painful—for a few hours, a few days, a week—but it was this very disappointment, this nothingness, which cleaned their minds for the next engagement. In her own distinct manner, it seemed to him, Mrs. Pugh exercised this profound detachment, though in her case it perhaps consisted of no more than a clear sense of priorities. She valued her independence, and would sacrifice the possibility of emotional ties with a man in order to maintain it. No, by every precept that he knew, she acquitted herself honorably. Each freedom required sacrifices, and Grange, though he might consider the matter from different perspectives, turning it this way and that on his pillow, could not but approve of her rationality.

And what of his own feelings? The casual predator rose from one meal and prepared himself without haste for the next. He was certain of one thing only, that his appetite would return. Yet he could not help but feel disquiet. Lying on his pillow, in the early hours, in the remembered radiance of warmth from his hostess's body, the conundrum teased him.

30

*S*he returned a little later to his room and, slipping into the unoccupied half of the bed, slept quietly by him. In his sleeping mind, he imagined that she returned out of a sense of loyalty or companionship, and guessed that this amiability would not violate her precepts about the Sabbath.

Yet when his fingers reached in the early morning toward her body, not out of lust but reassurance, she had already departed for church, leaving only a faint impression of warmth in the sheets. The light was already bright and birds sang as he stumbled drowsily to the washstand, poured cold water from a pitcher into the bowl, and began to wash.

On the chair his clothes were folded and arranged, and his valise carefully packed. This care and domesticity had a strange effect, half domestic, half erotic, as if she imparted the final caresses to his clothes. His shaver and brushes were laid beside the pitcher. Soaping his face, fragments of light seemed to move about him. Beginning to shave, he entered that state of contemplation in which men begin the day, gathering their selves together.

When he had shaved and dressed, he descended the oak staircase. At its base, Harrison issued from a side door like a long shadow.

"My mistress sends you her warmest wishes, and apologizes that she cannot meet you for breakfast. She bids you her fondest farewell, and a safe journey."

Harrison's air of seriousness was such as to command respect. Nodding to him in acknowledgment of his announcement, Grange experienced the faint impression of hunger under his ribs. As if he understood his guest's wishes, Harrison continued:

"Madam asked me to inform you that a breakfast hamper has been prepared for you in the carriage. My advice, sir, is that we should leave shortly if you wish to catch the early stage from Downton at eight fifteen."

"As you suggest." A thought occurred to Grange. "Did she not take the carriage herself?"

"She took the fly instead, sir. Madam likes to drive herself to church."

Half bowing briefly to Grange again, Harrison walked in front of him with stately grace, sliding back the locks of the main door, raising the great wooden cross-brace, and patiently waited for him to pass through.

The two-horse coach waited in the driveway. Grange mounted the step and Harrison closed the coach door behind him. The suspension swayed as Harrison swung up into the seat beside the driver. Almost immediately the driver called out and the horses surged.

In the heavily swaying compartment a wicker basket reposed on the main seat opposite. Beneath the covering awl, Grange found a leg of lamb, some cooked potatoes, a knife and fork. A fervent appetite gripped him, rising beneath his ribs, cold and sharp. Ignoring the knives and silver platter, he raised the leg of lamb to his mouth and, pausing momentarily, tore the meat directly with his teeth. His behavior surprised him, as a man may be surprised when someone else recalls an incident which he has forgotten. Eating was not so much a pleasure as the evisceration of appetite. As though he had lost his sense of detachment, he now merely gave in to his hunger.

Dining on the meat and eating from the soft flesh of the potato in the confined cage of the carriage, while the horses hooves thundered, he experienced something like a joy in the fleshly things. Beside the meat there was French wine, from a cellar laid down during the earlier years of peace with France. A terrible and calm abandon gripped him. He removed the cork of the bottle with his teeth, drank, and while he was so engaged (the branches of trees sweeping the carriage sides) it occurred to him that she would be seated or kneeling amongst penitents, taking Communion wine.

By the time he arrived at the outskirts of Downton, much of the cold excess of appetite had gone. He sat calmly in the carriage, staring straight ahead as he was delivered to the village.

Harrison stepped down, and carried Grange's valise to the stage stop.

"Thank you, Harrison. There is no need to wait."

"As you say, sir."

"You will return now?"

"Indeed, sir." Harrison turned toward him, as though to deliver a formal address. "Madam, before she departed to church, asked me to wish you a good journey."

"Thank you. Please convey my compliments in return."

"Goodbye, sir."

"Goodbye," Grange said.

Climbing up on the carriage beside the driver, Harrison turned to give a final, courteous inclination of the head, a gesture calculated for precise respect. The driver flicked the reins, and they drove off.

It was not the night that haunted him, but his memory of the garden. The rain began to fall, heavily, at first a few startled drops, then gathering weight suddenly they were in a downpour, laughing amongst the shrubs and flowers. Their first seizure over, they had collapsed on the grass. Yet the rain continued heavy on his back. Spreading her hair in rattails, he kissed her cheeks and neck, feeling beneath his lips the luminescence of her warmth. He removed his sodden jacket and shirt. Her fingers on his shoulders moved down the vertebrae. Her face had an unusual clarity, the clarity of lust or possession. Eyes, nose, mouth, the elemental landmarks; the face was the mask of the soul. Fleetingly, he observed something of himself in her eyes. It was this vision of himself which horrified him, that of a predator, a cold sensualist, moving about his rounds.

There are other images. Her whiteness moving parallel with her black shadow on the bedroom wall. The luminous glow on her hip, the hot darkness of her pubic hair. It is this that he feared, precisely this cold appreciation, the Minotaur in himself. He hoped perhaps that a love would one day save him from detachment. But what was proved appeared the opposite; that detachment will dissolve all love.

31

*R*eturned to Lymington, he spent much of the remainder of the day in correspondence and paperwork. Mrs. Thompson, after attending church, mended shirts in the kitchen below. Having achieved, after a few hours of application, the majority of his efforts, he drew down again from the shelves above his desk *A Treatise of Human Nature*.

In general we may remark, that the minds of men are mirrors to one another, not only because they reflect each other's emotions, but also because those rays of passions, sentiments and opinions may be often reverberated, and may decay away by insensible degrees. Thus the pleasure which a rich man receives from his possessions, being thrown upon the beholder, causes a pleasure and esteem; which sentiments again, being perceiv'd and sympathiz'd with, increase the pleasure of the possessor; and being once more reflected, become a new foundation for pleasure and esteem in the beholder. There is certainly an original satisfaction in riches derived from that power, which they bestow, of enjoying all the pleasures of life, and as this is their very nature and essence, it must be the first source of all the passions which arise from them. One of the most considerable of these passions is that of love or esteem in others, which therefore proceeds from a sympathy with the pleasure of the possessor. But the possessor has also a secondary satisfaction in riches arising from the love and esteem he acquires by them, and this satisfaction is nothing but a second reflexion of that original pleasure, which proceeded from himself. The secondary satisfaction or vanity becomes one of the principal recommendations of riches, and is the chief reason, why we either desire them for ourselves, or esteem them in others. Here then is a third rebound of the original pleasure, after which 'tis difficult to distinguish the images and reflexions, by reason of their faintness and confusion.

He ended his reading shortly afterward and, his thoughts full of the glittering mirror images of wealth, he replaced the book and took to the front door. Mrs. Thompson said:

"Are you out walking, sir?"

He turned and found her gazing upon him, holding in her hands a heavy cloak.

"It is variable weather, I think."

She had caught him squarely, neglecting the possibility of a downpour, and he allowed her to place the cloak over his shoulders and to do the catch, before nodding briskly to her and stepping outside into the overcast day.

His thoughts pursued him. He experienced a sense of unease, not only at the brilliance of the passage he had read, and the subtle means by which the great philosopher poured scorn on wealth, but in his own soul.

Neither, in his bed that night, could he sleep easily. He remembered Mrs. Pugh's house. Compared to his own narrow pallet, her bed was soft, the mattress was good, the pillows were stuffed with the finest eider feathers. Yet in honesty he was not drawn to luxury, to the flattering of the senses. No, it was his own role that concerned him, and how it had been changed. He would do what he could to help certain women toward fulfillment, toward what Mrs. Quill called "waking." But if Mrs. Pugh was to be the model of those to whom he should pay court, then it was clear she was already woken long ago, and he was merely one in a retinue of lovers. It was this which troubled him, which gave him a sense of disquiet.

His thoughts returned to Jane, whose image had risen in his mind. A complexity of emotions assailed him. He felt, in that area of deepest reserve which was his final refuge, that he had done what was necessary to see her. It was curious that his faith remained in Mrs. Quill, that he could not help but perceive her as benign. Did she merely demonstrate to him that of which he was capable? Yet he could not perceive her motive, and while it perplexed him, he was inclined out of instinct to grant her the benefit of the doubt. The result was that, more than ever, he felt under an obligation not to desecrate their agreement.

Several days later, when he was seated at his desk in his study, waiting for the first patient, Mrs. Thompson entered with a brief rap of knuckles on the door.

"Letter for you, sir."

"Thank you, Mrs. Thompson."

Her wide skirts brushed the doorframe as she departed, leaving the room like breath. He waited until her footsteps

had descended before, with thoughtful index finger, he opened
the letter.

> *Dear Silas,*
> *I heard from Mrs. Arabella Pugh that she greatly appreciated
> your visit.*
> *I am indebted for your consideration of our agreement.*
> *Perhaps you will call by for tea tomorrow. If you are unable to
> do so, please feel no need to reply. I shall be having tea at four o'
> clock, and I shall expect you only if I see you.*
> *Yours in gratitude,*
> *Celia Quill*

Placing the letter back in his pocket before Mrs. Thompson
reappeared in the doorway, he raised his eyes to her arrival.

"Are you ready to receive the first patient, sir?"

"Yes," Grange said. "Send him up directly."

He rose from his desk to greet the first patient of the day.

32

*I*n the calm glow of the afternoon light, Mrs. Quill closed
the door behind Grange, and paused.

"You look well, Silas, though perhaps a little thin."

"Thank you."

She wore a shift and gardening shoes, yet even in these she
seemed resplendent. A light from the hall window settled on
her cheek. She led him through to the drawing room, where

a tray of tea had already been placed, and invited him with all courtesy to be seated. To his eyes at least she appeared, in all outward character, remarkably composed. Carefully she poured, and he watched the faint down on her hands and wrists. In her presence he became lost in the particular, as in his own company he became absorbed in the abstract. She handed him a cup, smiled, and poured another for herself.

"Your visit gave Mrs. Pugh great comfort, Silas."

If Grange acknowledged her remark, it was with the minimum of affirmation, barely nodding.

"Yet," Mrs. Quill settled back, "do I detect that you yourself do not seem so pleased?"

"I have nothing to complain of, madam." He was inclined to watch her expression, but finding nothing there that would either encourage or discourage him, continued: "Yet even so, in some part of me I am disturbed."

She sipped her tea and considered him.

"Disturbed?"

"Mrs. Pugh, who I consider in many ways to be wise, made during dinner an interesting remark. She referred to her own religion, and to my lack of one, and said that it was I, not she, who struggled with my soul."

"You do not agree?" This was said with such simple clarity that for a moment Grange paused.

"On the contrary, madam, I know too well what she means. Lacking a God does not entail the loss of one's conscience. Indeed, without a God to guide and forgive, the struggle with the conscience becomes more terrible."

"My dear Silas, you are in melancholy mood. Did you, then, not enjoy her company?"

"Madam, she is attractive, honest, and amusing. How could I not?"

"Spoken gallantly. Yet you are still disturbed?"

"She also has the inestimable advantage of rendering unto God what is God's, and to Caesar what is due to Caesar."

Leaning forward to replace her cup, the sunlight touched her hair and seemed to strike a fiery vortex of golds and reds and pale ambers. He experienced the impression of observing heartfelt beauty, so that when she returned he watched, astonished at his lapse.

Perhaps Mrs. Quill caught something of his thought, for she smiled at his expression, and paused before speaking:

"And what disturbs you, then?"

"My conscience, madam. In my heart I do not feel that what I do is right."

" 'Right,' Silas, is a very dangerous word." He was surprised at the underlying fierceness of her response, and watched her compose herself, before she continued: "It binds women to men in marriage and in slavery. Mrs. Pugh and Mrs. Boxer, my good friends, have chosen to live their lives as they see fit, not according to some notion of right which is alien to them." She looked upon him directly, without equivocation. "Is it that, perhaps, which disturbs you?"

"No, madam, it is not that which disturbs me. It is, rather, my own response."

"How so?"

"I cannot find a rational reason for feeling as I do. The day that I returned, I felt this strange abandon, as if what was heavy had left me."

"That troubles you?"

"Yes."

She studied him without expression.

"Silas, you are a fine young man. You do not think you are handsome, yet you are attractive. You have attributes of charm, intelligence, and fine manners. If you could find it in yourself to abandon your struggle with your conscience, you would perhaps be happy."

Aware of the quality of silence, its living depths, he searched for words.

"If I abandoned my conscience, madam, I do not know what I would be."

"Perhaps," Mrs. Quill suggested calmly, "you would be free."

She paused, drank her tea, replaced her cup. He watched

her expression—which it seemed to him could suggest nothing or everything by turns—now compose itself to one of purest generosity and concern.

"I know that I have no right over your life. But if you refused the struggle with your conscience, these strong-minded, independent women would become your protectors and champions." She smiled. "They would advance your career. More than this, they would teach you much about life that you do not know. They would bring you out of your dry study."

"Madam, the more I learn about what you call life, the more I do believe that I am not fit for it."

Mrs. Quill put down her teacup with an audible click.

"Perhaps you are not the man I took you for. You would prefer to return to your bachelor's life with your cold books?"

"No, madam. I would like to marry your daughter, and settle to a life in matrimony."

He gained the impression of a deepening silence; more than this, of some barrier being raised. Her face did not move, but a distinct coldness seemed to move around her.

"That is impossible. She is already married."

"Unless she is devout of the Church of Rome, there is separation. I would support her well . . ."

"You should not even think of it."

In spite of the coldness that descended between them, he was determined to continue.

"A moment ago, you derided my bachelor's life. Yet when I make it clear that my intentions are to pursue a course of marriage, you act to prevent me."

Something seemed to rise inside her, something stubborn and profound. Now Mrs. Quill stood up and calmly walked the full extent of the room away from him, pausing at its furthest extremity to look outward into the garden, until she turned at the other end. "We must speak of this no more."

Grange too raised himself to his feet. "You gave an undertaking, madam. If I visited Mrs. Pugh, you would allow me to see your daughter again."

"It is impossible." Spoken with such clarity, he found himself disposed more than ever against implacable will. Even so, something in him cried out.

"You promised, madam!"

"I gave you an understanding, sir, that if you showed yourself independent of your infatuation by visiting Mrs. Pugh, I would consider the matter."

"I did so . . ."

"Instead, I find that this same infatuation on your part is strengthened, and that you have merely used Mrs. Pugh to obtain access to my daughter."

"Madam . . ."

"You must leave, sir, now."

If he had hesitated until then, her movement now toward the door was so icy, so firm, he was compelled to obey her. He followed, angry but containing himself.

At the door he swung toward her, but Mrs. Quill forestalled him.

"Good-day, sir."

He hovered on the edge of speech, and would have spoken, but a glance at her face showed no trace of weakness or charity. There was a sense in which he knew his efforts would be to no purpose.

"Good-day, madam."

The door closed firmly behind him. Or rather, foreclosed. It was not slammed directly, but with a calm, emphatic force that seemed to strike its sparks into his soul. Locks were drawn. He had never known such a terrible sound, as if the tumblers were his own heart, wrenched into rigid silence. She was his jailer, but was locking him out. He felt the shudder of his despair. He walked down the path. He closed the iron gate behind him. There was no one in the little lane outside. Out of sight of the house, he felt weak and leaned against the wall. Then, gathering himself with an effort, he began to walk back to his house.

Yet in the anguished considerations which now overcame him, which were released by his situation, he retained sufficient presence of mind to consider that the prospect of returning in his present state would alarm Mrs. Thompson, and he would be subject to the added distress of her own close scrutiny and inevitable interrogation as to the cause of his discomfort. Accordingly, he proceeded to make his way toward the foreshore, in the hope that there he might recover some of his composure—enough at least to pass by his housekeeper without raising the fury of her suspicion concerning his good sense.

If he was in turmoil, the day itself exhibited no such pattern. The sun had already fallen, and a calm dusk had appeared above the waters.

33

On the foreshore, he peered out across the silent marshes. In the calm dusk he observed several of the gray herons standing as calm as sentinels.

Though he might come on them unawares, yet they seemed to know his presence, and to merely continue their calm, absorbed lives. They lived at the edge of water; if he were called upon to expose his deeper thoughts, he fancied they inhabited some other medium, at the edge of his own and other human consciousness. They might have been visionaries in their own peculiar and private world. He liked them for their deliberate footsteps, their concentration as they peered into the depths of ponds and water edges, their remote sidelong glance, like an academic disturbed when reading.

Sometimes, flying low, they seemed merely part of the landscape, a flat object parallel with the horizon, that lived only a shadow's brief depth above the level of water. Yet on landing, folding the slow wing, he had a strange intuition that death was life's completion, that he had nothing to fear beyond it.

"Sir." Mrs. Thompson stared at him. "You are as white as a sheet."

She examined him from the open doorway. Grange did his best to hide his perturbation, though the slight shaking of his hands as he took off his boots perhaps gave him away.

"I feel tolerable."

Mrs. Thompson appeared dubious.

"You seem ill, sir. Do you have a chill?"

"I believe I may have the first traces of a fever," Grange replied. She handed him his undershoes. He put them on, stood up, and turned to go upstairs.

Aware perhaps that she could not press him further, another thought now rose in her.

"I was asked to tell you immediately on your return, sir. Dr. Hargood called. He seemed concerned. He wished to speak with you as soon as possible."

About to ascend the first step, Grange turned again to face her.

"He hoped you might call by at his house. He left this letter."

"Thank you, Mrs. Thompson." He looked directly into her eyes, and for a moment it seemed that she challenged his authority, that the severity of her gaze penetrated his defenses; her expression suggested overseeing of his affairs gave her this right. "That will be all."

Mrs. Thompson gave him a final appraising glance, then her eyes turned away reluctantly from his. After she had departed, Grange opened the letter.

> *Silas, my dear fellow,*
> *I received a missive from London today. I have some important and urgent news for you concerning a matter we discussed at our recent dinner.*
> *Please call by at my house as soon as you return from your walk.*
> *Yours as ever,*
> *Hargood*

He washed his face in the handbasin, though he avoided glancing at himself in the mirror, as though he knew what he saw would merely confirm his distress. In the calm ceremony of washing and drying his hands he always found solace. Yet, touching his face inadvertently during drying, the coldness of his fingers transmitted to his mind an impression of detachment from his body, a distance from its mildest sensations.

Having washed, he set out a second time that evening, walking down Lymington Hill toward the river. Crossing the tollbridge, he was again impressed by the sensations of his body, the rub of a heel inside one boot, the sound of his own breath as if from another person. He passed the foreshore but did not pause to gaze out at its singular gray denizens. He struck inland, following the bridle path that formed the most direct route to Hargood's house, arriving there in the cool of dusk. A lamp had already been lit and hung beside the door on a metal hook, though there was still daylight enough to see. At his second knock the catch was drawn almost violently, the door flung open, and Hargood, both animated and serious, appeared there.

"Silas, my dear man."

Hargood flung a heavy arm over his shoulder, and together they went inside into the sitting room. In front of the great fireplace, Hargood lowered his arm and swung to face him.

"It is good to see you. You look weak, sir. Sit down."

"Thank you. I feel reasonable enough."

Hargood moved toward the mantel above the fireplace, as though it commanded the room, turned to face him again, and laid an arm along the ledge, as if to steady himself.

"I heard from my mistress again. A letter arrived this morning. The charming creature writes to me almost every day. During my absence she remembered something about the name of Quill. What I am about to tell you may come as a shock." Hargood halted and looked at him directly. "I did not mean it to be so."

Watching Hargood pause, Grange began to feel a terrible presentiment. It was not that which Hargood said, but his demeanor, which seemed calculated to put his guest at ease, but whose seriousness, rather, had the opposite effect—of placing his fear at attention.

"She remembers the name Quill because it featured prominently in a scandal several years ago. I cannot be certain that it refers to the same person, but in my heart I feel it is connected. Would you like some wine, dear fellow?" Hargood asked suddenly. "You look pale."

"No, thank you," Grange replied.

Hargood glanced at him with a certain closeness of inspection and then, only partly satisfied, began again. "The account she remembered was this. There are a number of establishments where men with money go to spend leisure hours with young women. As you know, these vary from certain low houses for whores to other establishments that have a certain surface refinement, but that purvey the same merchandise.

"In the news sheets several years ago, there was an account of one such establishment. It was a refined house of the type I mentioned. It came to light, however, that the precise nature of this establishment was different from others. It was a respectable frontage, to be sure—a well-kept residence in Cheyne Walk. However, it seemed that, behind a facade of the utmost gentility, the house provided certain young men for the entertainment of rich women." Hargood paused and coughed to clear his throat, and delivered his next sentence conversationally. "It was owned by a certain Mrs. Quill."

Grange experienced a sense of suspension, as though he floated in space. Then, as if to fill the space caused by the arrest of his senses, he began to hear a thudding in his head and to feel a heated sensation in his skin. Yet these were mere physical aberrations. In his mind he could not believe for a moment that the two were connected. In the absence of response, he bit his lip and, seeking to control his reply, waited.

Hargood was clearly set upon continuing, for to halt now would have been merciless indeed. "You know what these places are like. If put down, or suppressed, in due course they will turn up somewhere else. There was a prosecution, but nothing could be proved. The proprietress conducted herself with considerable dignity, by all accounts, and so impressed the jury that she departed from the court scot-free, though with her reputation somewhat tarnished. She disappeared, temporarily at least, from the London scene. The rumor was that she had retired to the provinces to allow time to heal, and would return."

Grange heard himself speak as if from a distance:

"Are you suggesting Mrs. Quill is the same person?"

Yet Hargood would not answer directly. In matters of the heart he displayed the sure instincts of an advocate.

"Perhaps," he commented, "I may report merely what I heard and leave deduction up to you as you see fit. It is perhaps merely a coincidence of names. But there was a further aspect. The young men who were supplied by the establishment were not merely taken off the streets. They were . . . refined, often of good backgrounds, and could charm their rich female clients."

"Hargood," Grange whispered, "I cannot listen further . . ."

"Silas, concentrate your mind, I beg you, on one more detail. In the prosecution of this house, the means by which one young man was entrapped created surprise. This same young man gave evidence for the prosecution. He claimed that the proprietress—Mrs. Quill—introduced him to a charming young woman who she claimed was her daughter. In fact the girl was herself a strumpet, an attractive one to be sure, part of Mrs. Quill's variegated household. The young man fell in love, but Mrs. Quill refused to allow him to see her so-called daughter until he had carried out an agreement to offer his services to certain of her rich, female clientele."

Grange uttered a cry and stood up. He felt faint. Hargood, abandoning his position at the mantel, moved forward to support him.

"Silas, my dear man. Sit down. I know this must be terribly distressing. I apologize. Are you sure you wouldn't like some wine?"

Grange sat collapsed in his chair, his face in his hands.

"Damn me," Hargood said, "I am afraid there was nothing I could do but warn you." He paused again. "Damn me, what a business. Damn me!"

Hargood walked to the sideboard. He poured wine out of a decanter into a large glass. He returned to Grange, insisted he take the drink. Grange did not look at him, but after further encouragement he accepted the glass and drank.

34

*G*range was unable to recall the journey back. The wine seemed to deaden his senses, but his determination to depart as soon as possible increased with his terror of sudden collapse. Hargood prevailed upon him to stay, and to accept further hospitality for the night, but his stomach rejected the notion of a meal vehemently. He was set upon leaving before he betrayed his deepest anguish. Despite Hargood's protestations that he should not walk, that he should allow his host to drive him back in the brougham, Grange was able to walk toward the hallway and to make a good show of being in sound mind.

Even so, Hargood, anxiously following him through the hall, said, "Silas, I should walk with you. You are too distressed to be alone."

"There is no need, I assure you."

"It is my responsibility that you are struck down."

"The air will do me good."

"It is becoming dark. You look so weak, sir, you will fall into a ditch, if you do not throw yourself into it."

Grange's white face glimmered in the gloom. "I see well enough in the dark, Hargood. It is in plain light that I cannot see."

Mrs. Thompson called "Sir," as he blundered past her and walked up the stairs, without removing his walking boots, and when he did not pause, called again "Sir!"

She heard the door close, his feet drag across the floorboards, and then the sigh of chair legs scraping the floor as he sank into his chair.

A Treatise of Human Nature lay on the desk, still open. With a great effort he began to read to himself aloud, slowly, like a child:

> *As to the influence of contiguity and resemblance, we may observe, that if the contiguous and resembling object be comprehended in this system of realities, there is no doubt but these two relations will assist that of cause and effect, and infix the related idea with more force in the imagination. Even where the related object is but feigned, the relation will serve to enliven the idea, and increase its influence. A poet, no doubt, will be the better able to form a strong description of the Elysian fields, that he prompts his imagination by the view of a beautiful meadow or garden; as at another he may, by his fancy, place himself in the midst of these fabulous regions, that by the feigned contiguity he may enliven his imagination. . . .*

The text was obscured by the cloud of his own thoughts. He could go no further. He was overcome by tiredness and his face sank forward onto the cold pages of the open book.

The following morning, Hargood and Mrs. Thompson stood by Grange's bed.

Mrs. Thompson said, "I am sorry to call you, sir. I found him yesterday evening, at his desk, slumped over. I helped him to bed, but he's been in a fever all night, sweating and calling out in his sleep. I watched over him."

"You did well, Mrs. Thompson."

In his deliberation, Hargood moved to the side of Grange's bed and placed his hand against Grange's cheek.

"He is ill?" Mrs. Thompson's eyes studied Hargood across the bed. He perceived in their depths her shrewd intelligence, and the force of her concern.

"It is a humor, an affliction of the mind or of the imagination."

"His mind is afflicted?"

"Yes, his mind is afflicted, though he is not mad." Hargood paused, then added, "But it might be best if we treated him as if he were."

"Sir . . . ?"

"Add to this, that mind and body are part of the same. We shall need to treat the two together, since the affliction of both mind and body is produced by the one cause."

"You know the cause, sir?"

"Yes, the ostensible cause. It is something which he must come to terms with, in his own time. In the meantime, I am going to bleed him."

He looked across the bed at Mrs. Thompson. She studied him with an intensity that in other circumstances he would have found unsettling. Watching her observe him thus, he felt she deserved some explanation greater than the mere reiteration of a physician's authority.

"He is as strong as an ox, and he is driven by terrible remorse. If we allow him, he will be up in his fever and about, in great distress and anguish. I shall bleed him enough to keep him to his bed. Do you understand what I say?"

Mrs. Thompson nodded slowly, as though overcoming her own fear.

"I believe so, sir."

"I tell you this because it is you who will look after him."

"You ask my permission, sir? I trust you."

"No. I will do what I believe is necessary on my own authority. I merely warn you that afterward he will be listless. In the meantime, I intend to render his body as weak as is necessary, so the physical recovery will grant sufficient time for his mind to rest."

"Sir . . ."

"That is what I intend. He must shed enough blood as though it were a great wound. Then we must hope that the mind and the body will heal in parallel."

"You need my help, sir?"

"Not directly. I shall cut an artery, and then bind it. In the meantime, I shall want several jugs for the blood."

"I will fetch them, sir."

"Mrs. Thompson."

Mrs. Thompson turned.

"While this illness lasts, send all his patients on to me. I'll deal with them. He needs a long rest. Several weeks at least. Now, if you would also boil me some water."

Mrs. Thompson departed. In her absence Hargood raised a wooden case onto the table they had together placed beside the bed. He opened a lid, within which was revealed an interior full of knives and medical implements. Turning toward Grange, he whispered, more in pity than in anger:

"Silas, you damned wise fool, with your head full of learning . . ."

Carefully he laid out several knives on the bare table.

35

At the foot of Grange's bed, Mrs. Thompson sewed carefully, drawing the thread through the pattern with long strokes
of her plump arm. Her eyes drifted occasionally toward
Grange, asleep. She had taken off her linen cap and set it
beside her. Her hair, uncovered, showed gray amongst the
gold hairs. Behind her bowed head, the curtain was drawn
against excessive sun in the west-facing room.

Not long after half past four in the afternoon Grange stirred and opened his eyes. Mrs. Thompson put her sewing aside, rose, went to the head of the bed, looked down at him.

"You seem a little better, sir."

Several moments passed, it seemed to her, before a sense of realization entered his eyes. His face was white, a line of sweat visible on his upper lip. As his memories came back, so he closed his eyes again.

"My patients . . ."

"Dr. Hargood is taking care of them," Mrs. Thompson said. "He says you have to rest." She paused, then added gently, "Dr. Hargood's instructions, sir."

She was aware that the phrase "Dr. Hargood's instructions," given the robust relationship between the two physicians, would normally occasion amusement. But not the faintest trace of a smile appeared on Grange's face. Instead, as if in pain, he turned away and closed his eyes.

"You must let me shave you, sir."

Grange made no comment, propped against the headboard of the bed. Mrs. Thompson placed a pillow under his head and applied the warm lather to his stubbled cheek, then she began, slowly at first, to use the razor with unexpected expertise. The very business of consideration seemed to oppress him. It was as if life was a form of pretense, or at least something which did not bear the cost of energy. Mrs. Thompson had drawn up a chair. Under her concentration, the razor moved across his cheek, his jaw, his throat. With facecloth and towel she wiped the remaining traces of soap and water from his face.

"I should like to sit at the window," Grange said.

"You are still feverish, sir. I feel it on your cheeks."

"The window," Grange repeated, as if the fever had burned out everything except his will.

Whether her compliance was a loss of her power, or whether he was so frail and so much in her power that she gave in to his wishes out of sympathy, she agreed to help him to the window. In a chair, a blanket over him, Grange sat looking out of his study over the meadows, toward the Solent.

At seven thirty Mrs. Thompson, entering the room, asked: "Would you like something to eat, sir?"

"No, thank you."

Mrs. Thompson glanced at his still back, at the composure of his head and neck, then left. He remained without moving while the light changed slowly and the shadows rose slowly up the wall, until Hargood appeared beside him. Though he might have been expecting Hargood's entrance, Grange barely acknowledged his presence. His visitor, notwithstanding, drew up a chair and sat down alongside him. Eventually, Hargood said, "Silas, I paid a visit to Mrs. Quill earlier today. I took the liberty of informing her that you were ill."

"Hargood . . ." Grange's voice was hoarse, and Hargood detected, for once, a note almost of pleading.

But Hargood pressed on. "You must listen to me, sir. She showed concern and enquired after you closely . . . I took the opportunity of informing her also that I had heard of a certain Mrs. Quill who had removed herself from London following a scandal . . ." Hargood waited, wondering how much of what he said would reach his friend and patient, how much would be excluded. "She is an extraordinary woman. Someone other would have denied it, avoided it, turned away, allowed herself some privacy of thought. But she looked at me directly, as bold and unafraid as a tiger, and said that she was the same woman. There was no reproach in her eyes toward me. Even so, I felt I had transgressed her hospitality. She accompanied me to the door, without a word. I bid her a formal goodbye, and I left."

In the silence that followed, Grange closed his eyes.

Hargood said, "Silas, it is best to settle this, to allow no further room for doubt. A glimmer of hope will merely prolong your illness. It will be like a blade which, once it has entered, works its way into the body's core."

Grange did not respond. After a few seconds, Hargood stood to leave.

"I must attend to my patients," Hargood said. "You will send a message by Mrs. Thompson if you need me. I will call by again tomorrow evening."

Grange merely nodded, more perhaps to dismiss Hargood's presence than to acknowledge the contents of his speech. After a few moments Hargood's footsteps moved down the stairs.

Working in the kitchen below, scouring several heavy cooking pots, Mrs. Thompson heard Hargood close the door, and shortly afterward the rumble of wheels as his brougham moved off along the street. She paused and looked up toward the ceiling, but she heard nothing from Grange's study. After a few seconds she continued with her scouring.

Entering his room perhaps an hour and a half later, Mrs. Thompson found him the same. As night came on, Grange continued to stare out of the window at the gray water beyond the marshes, at the changing, folding light. Not long after ten, Mrs. Thompson insisted that he return to bed, and Grange, lacking the will to resist, allowed her to help him across the bare floorboards.

The following evening, Mrs. Thompson again opened the door to Hargood, laid his cloak over the banister, and from her customary position at the stairwell watched him as he walked upstairs.

Grange was in the same attitude as the previous evening, staring out of the window. For several seconds, Hargood stood beside him.

He drew up a chair and sat down beside his patient, so that he too faced the dusk. Like Grange, he became aware of the luminous surface of the water, the movement of light.

"How are you feeling, my dear fellow?"

Grange nodded weakly. "I appreciate what you've done for me, Hargood, I really do."

Hargood sat quietly for several seconds.

"You were in love with the girl she introduced as her daughter?"

Grange stared out to sea, and Hargood was forced to follow his gaze again. On the Solent the night drew the light downward toward the surface of the water, toward the meniscus of the horizon. Hargood spoke directly, as if to the sea and the changing light:

"I learned something more about the matter, Silas. The young man who accused Mrs. Quill of running a house . . . He later admitted that the girl Jane, with whom he was enamored, was in fact Mrs. Quill's real daughter. There was a complication in proving the fact absolutely. Mrs. Quill refused to name the father, but that is a detail . . ." Hargood paused, gathered himself, and spoke again to the blind light. "I think perhaps in that respect at least Mrs. Quill is exonerated."

Grange did not speak, and Hargood wondered, not for the first time, whether he had ceased to listen and had entered his own private world. In the absence of response, he nevertheless felt compelled to continue:

"In telling you of the case as reported in the *Courier*, I owe you an apology. One should not believe news sheets. I do acknowledge that the truth is nearly always more complex than we are at first inclined to believe. In a case such as this, it is easily lost in claim and counterclaim. The only thing that is certain, I believe, is that we will never know the full ramifications of this matter."

Grange was silent. Only the spaces of the room seemed to observe Hargood's sentences. Having driven this far, he felt compelled to continue. "Yet it is also true that once one part of the story is found to be false, one begins to doubt the other aspects. I should never have transmitted the story to you in its first and crudest form. I should have guessed your state of mind, and desisted. I told you once I believe that woman is outstandingly honest. I never was more impressed by anyone."

So it was left. Grange declined to reply. Perhaps twenty minutes later Hargood rose and, without acknowledgment from Grange, left the room. Mrs. Thompson heard the creak of the stairs as he descended, and was at the banister like a ghost to hand the physician his gloves and cloak. Hargood nodded to her, but did not speak.

36

*T*he following evening, when Hargood returned again to consider the health of his patient, Mrs. Thompson waited at the bottom of the stairs while he ascended. She was still there when, about to close the door of the study, he glanced down to see her face in the gloom of the stairwell, turned up toward him like a white lily in water.

He closed the door, drew up a chair to sit beside Grange, and stared out at the changing light. Yet it was Grange who spoke first, unexpectedly, in a voice depleted of energy.

"Since you exonerate Mrs. Quill, Hargood, I exonerate you."

"Silas . . ."

Grange struggled again to speak:

"Everything you did, you did to protect me."

Disarmed suddenly, Hargood experienced an unexpected confusion of his own emotions. "You were, or are, in love with the daughter. I have caused a terrible interruption . . ."

He studied his patient. Grange was so severely agitated by thought that his hand shook, and his frame seemed to writhe under the pressure of his emotion. Hargood gained the impression that Grange was attempting to convey something that distressed him, that he formed his words carefully.

"It is a strange thing . . . I do not think I was in love with Jane. Perhaps I deluded myself. I think it was Mrs. Quill that I felt something for . . . I sense that in some way I have let her down."

"Silas, you must not . . ."

Grange paused again, gathering the strength to speak.

"I have let her down, Hargood. In the depths of my heart, I know it."

"It is that which will prevent your recovery, my dear Silas. Guilt is a terrible contagion. It is worse than sympathy."

Hargood visited the following evening, visited and left. Mrs. Quill's name was not mentioned, as if a truce held between them. Several evenings later, on his daily visit, Hargood felt the occasion to speak to Grange of a matter that he regarded as private.

"Silas, I am a widower, as you know. Yet you have never heard me speak of my wife, much though I loved her, and much happiness I sustained with her. The reason is simple. I do not dwell on the past. And the reason I do not is that happiness, by its own nature, breeds no regret. I merely make a point. Listen, sir, if you can, because it is one of the few things of use, the very few, that I am able to impart.

"I will tell you something, Silas. It is my experience that, in the main, people do not grieve over the loss of happiness. Those who have experienced it know in their hearts that it is a gift, and that to grieve over its loss is somehow to tarnish that gift. I have observed that those who grieve most terribly are those who suffered the most. I do not understand fully why this is so, but in my experience at least it is proven beyond doubt. Perhaps it is because they grieve over the lost possibility. Perhaps they long for the happiness that might have been. Life is unfair. Those who suffer most in relationships are struck down again by remorse when they are finished.

"I am inchoate. I do not have your clarity of perception. But experience is something; it teaches a few, simple things. That is why you must forget Mrs. Quill and her daughter. You must forget them for your own good. Perhaps you learned something from them. Perhaps you learned something about yourself. Take what small benefit you can, and when you have done so, forget the rest. Forget the rest as soon as you are able, and then your mind will recover."

Hargood waited, but Grange did not respond. In due course, he stood up to go. As he was about to leave, he sensed suddenly that Grange might speak:

"Hargood, tell me one thing. I am as weak as a kitten. How much blood did you take?"

"Enough, sir. Enough to give you a certain time in which to allow your mind to repair."

"You assumed," Grange said, "I would dismember myself, and so you have removed the source of my energy."

"Sunlight is like pain. It inflicts its brightness and only in the darkness will the eye recover. Darkness and shadow are a respite."

"Hargood . . ."

Hargood could sense the onset of exhaustion, but Grange was determined to make a point.

"You yourself should feel no guilt."

Hargood hovered, tempted to speak further, but an unexplained gratitude at these few words rose upward, and he left the room quietly, abandoning his patient to his vigil by the window.

The following evening, Mrs. Thompson at the door appeared robust as usual. Hargood was not absolved of his own guilt, but it seemed to him that for the time being it could be set aside. He looked for the first time into her face, observing there the depths of her anguish, concerned that in his absorption he had failed to perceive a simple fact; that while he considered the plight of his patient, she took care of two patients.

"He begins to eat, sir."

"And you?" Hargood asked. "You eat enough?"

She was surprised at his question, and doubt at the answer filled her eyes. To deflect attention from this strangeness, he turned the subject once again to his patient.

"In his mind, too, he seems better."

He might have wept at the relief in her face.

Mrs. Thompson said, "He seems more his old self."

"He needs to replace lost blood. Give him red meat if you can, roasted, not boiled, to preserve the salt."

"I give him fish broth, for the time being, sir. Red meat he cannot yet keep down."

Hargood found himself at a loss. She was looking into his face, with that concentration and detachment he found uncomfortable.

"I would thank you, Mrs. Thompson, if it were not impertinent."

She continued to regard him. He knew, or guessed, what she observed there—the perturbation of emotion that is not allowed to find an outlet. There was no insolence in her stare. Rather, she watched him out of innocence, like a child at a fair who observes something magical and extraordinary. Hargood, the great rake, his jaw hardened against emotion as if against pain, stood in front of her in unexpected discomposure, unable to retreat out of pride, a tear moving down the heavy bone of his cheek.

Having stood his ground enough, he nodded as if to dismiss her, though in reality he dismissed himself. She watched from the stairwell as he made his way up the stairs, knocked on the bedroom door and, accustomed to hearing no answer, entered.

Grange was seated in the wicker chair, sleeping. A blanket had been set over him, and part trailed on the floorboards. There was something active in his breathing. Hargood, still coughing quietly to himself out of embarrassment, observed the pallor of his patient's face. There was no color there, but the thin clamminess which had clung to his skin since the fever began seemed to have retreated. Finding himself unobserved, Hargood drew the back of his hand across his cheek to remove the trace of his emotion, cast his eyes around, lifted a chair quietly, set it down again beside and a little behind Grange, then sat down and composed himself for a vigil.

Perhaps half an hour later, Mrs. Thompson knocked quietly at the door and enquired in low voice whether Hargood required tea. He nodded his assent, searching her face briefly for some trace of his weakness; but instead Mrs. Thompson gave him a look of pure respect, which discomfited him slightly.

Grange continued to breathe regularly in sleep. A few minutes later, Mrs. Thompson set down the tray on a table, and left.

At length Grange stirred, swallowed, and after a pause spoke out to the shadow beside him.

"Hargood, you catch me asleep."

"Do not feel obliged to speak, Silas, or to reply." Hargood waited several seconds while Grange gathered his senses, before continuing. "Your forgiveness emboldens me. I have a second cause for apology. You said once, on a different occasion, that all that was necessary for evil in the world was two differing views of the human good. Mrs. Quill's and mine are different. Yet somehow we have contrived, between us, almost to crush you."

He had become used to Grange's pauses, while he mustered energy in his mind, which, like his body, seemed drained of blood to answer. Grange's voice rasped thinly: "You believe she was well intentioned?"

Hargood nodded, as much to himself as to Grange. Seated side by side in the twilight.

"You consider, no doubt, how she maneuvered you. I do not know the details, nor would I wish you to disclose them. But remember that no one knows his or her own heart entirely, not even a woman such as Mrs. Quill. If we are lucky, we learn as we progress. I am inchoate as usual. I say, perhaps in her way, she is not entirely sure of what she does."

Grange showed no reaction. Hargood continued:

"Before I leave, I have one more thing to report. Mrs. Quill has left her house. Yesterday her luggage and effects were put aboard a stage. I do not know her destination, and it is not my intention to enquire . . ."

Perhaps it was the set of Grange's head, or the look of impassivity that returned to his face, the eyes particularly, which caused Hargood to sense that his attention had wandered, or that he had retired to some private domain.

Mrs. Thompson helped Grange to his bed. As he shuffled across the oak floors, he leaned on her ample shoulders and strong frame. She drew off his trousers and helped him with his shirt. Breathing with the effort, she glanced down at him. Lying in bed, he stared up into her eyes without expression. The light darkened as the night drew on.

In the morning light, Mrs. Thompson helped Grange to dress. His fever had finally receded and he had gained some strength. He leaned on her shoulder as he moved to the chair. She left him staring out of the window.

Mrs. Thompson stood beside him with a tray of food, fish

broth and a plate of warmed slices of roast beef, as Hargood
had suggested. But though he would eat the broth, Grange
refused the beef with a calm sense of purpose, as if his will was
developing its force once again, and was expressing itself, if
not in negation, then against Hargood's absolute jurisdiction.
Mrs. Thompson's footsteps receded down the stairs.

After shaving the following morning, Grange insisted again
that he should take up his position by the window. The same
was true the following day, and the day after. Mrs. Thompson, knowing him to be a person of strong habit, observed
slow but continual progress in his strength; that he now shaved
himself without her help, that he could move about the room
increasingly without her support.

Close by midday, toward the end of the second week of his
illness, the Telegraph stagecoach halted in front of the house.
Its leather blinds were removed by the groom and its heavy
door swung open. A single man emerged, then a few seconds
later another man, his wife, two children.

Grange hardly registered their faces, lost in his own
thoughts. Now a third person, a single woman, stepped free
of the carriage and for a second glanced up the street into the
sun. She wore a heavy cloak and a broad hat. Yet there was
something familiar about her as she began to walk away, a
curious confidence and discretion in her gait.

For the first time, perhaps, in his position of recuperation at
the window, a sign of strong animation entered Grange's face.
He leaned forward, coughing, to view her progress. Walking
steadily, she moved out of his line of sight. He whispered,
mouthed to himself:

"Jane."

It might not be, but it was precisely this possibility that
now stirred him. Stung into attention, yet under the suspicion
that he was suffering a delusion, he felt his body, for all its
weakness, grow tense. It was this same terror that seemed to
cause him to writhe inward and upward, like an eel, holding
onto the sill for support. He gained a temporary footing and

stood with difficulty, swayed, regained his balance. The room swirled like water. In his commiseration, he was unsteady on his feet. He opened the door of his study, listened, and began to edge as quietly as he could down the stairs, pausing between each step, leaning on the wall for support. Silence rose toward him, a silence inhabited by tension.

Was Mrs. Thompson listening? He paused in the hallway for several seconds, pale with the effort in his attenuated state. Mrs. Thompson in the kitchen now seemed a series of clear but distant sounds, her soul a simple energy in motion; the clatter of dishes, the rattle of cutlery.

Easing open the door, Grange stepped outside, drawing the catch closed quietly. It was one thing to stare out of a darkened room into a sunlit street, another to place the body's exhausted surfaces in the open air. To his fevered eyes, the sun was preternaturally bright beneath its hall of fire. He put his hand up against the bright glare. A hundred yards away he observed a figure which might have been Jane turn a corner and then, in brisk but gliding motion, walk swiftly into the sun's shadow.

37

*T*here was a stream of traffic in the High Street, which seemed like the steady trickle of water. Though he might not usually notice it, today it seemed to hold him back from his course. Setting off with an unsteady walk, Grange struggled to stay upright, leaning against buildings while he gathered himself.

The first part of his journey was downhill, to the causeway and tollbridge. Having gained the opposite bank, he paused for several minutes at the riverside before he began to climb the hill, then, with greater effort, slowly ascended the quiet lane that led to Mrs. Quill's house. A fit of coughing, combined with dizziness, took him at the juncture with Barrows Lane, and he was forced to wait until his senses returned. At her garden gate, he paused again, breathing heavily. Then he walked up the path, paused in front of the porch, and raised the doorknocker, letting it fall, coughing in the silence that now enveloped him.

There was no reply. He applied some weight, half leaning on the jamb, but the door was locked. Turning round, he placed his back against the door and, struggling for breath, looked around him.

The garden had a deserted appearance, as if the human hand had, by small degrees, withdrawn its hold. Weeds grew over the edges of the brick pathways and began to make their appearance in the roses. The wind had drawn down a creeper from a side wall, and it had not been replaced. These small elements of neglect formed into a picture of desertion.

He began to make his way around the house, his hand tracing the walls. Forced to pause several times against the brickwork, he found in due course a second garden gate. It was locked with an old chain. He leaned against it, assembling what little pressure he could. It held, though as force was loaded, it creaked and complained. Gathering the remnants of his will, he pushed against it. The chain groaned and then, as if in deep reluctance, gave with a sigh; he barely managed to restrain himself falling headlong into the smaller rear garden.

Regaining his balance, he felt his way along the further wall to the house's back door, pausing there to gather his strength, and tried the door. It seemed securely bolted. He tested it with his shoulder as much as he was able, but it showed no signs of movement. He leaned backward against the door, and was about to return by the way he came when he noticed, by virtue of his resting position, perhaps seven or eight inches upward from the eye's natural trajectory, a small item that protruded from a crack in the brickwork. When he raised his glance to consider it more closely, it became a piece of waste string. He raised his fingers to it and withdrew, with a brief scraping of metal tones on the brick, a solid brass key that was attached to it. He was forced to pause again before the next stage. Fitted to the lock, under its impulsion the door opened easily.

Inside the scullery, his breathing was labored, heavy. He moved into the hall and observed, with a fearfulness that now bordered on fatalism, the emptiness of the rooms. There were several chests and cases packed by a wall. Apart from these few items, the last vestiges of evacuation, there was no furniture. The house was empty. It was the final import that Mrs. Quill was leaving, or had left already, that her leaving was an accomplished fact.

The sitting room, too, echoed without its furniture. Discovering nothing there to hold his attention, he moved back into the hall. A fit of coughing took hold of his lungs, and his knees felt weak. He was about to collapse when he heard, behind his own wheezing, a faint sound somewhere on an upper floor.

Yet as he began to move up the stairs, one by one, holding to the banister with one hand for support, he felt the swirl of weakness, the dark waters rising. He clutched at his chest, swayed, reached out with both hands for the banister. To collapse here would be dangerous. He knew that to ascend further was beyond him, and now retreated down the stairs slowly, conserving his energy, until he reached the ground floor. There he paused again.

He was about to faint. The hammerings of his heart caught up with him. A sweat broke out on his body. It seemed to him that the final traces of the blood he had lost ebbed away from him. There was an abandoned trunk in the hall, adjacent the closer wall, and he slowly slid down the wall until he was sitting on it. He leaned back against the wall and closed his eyes.

Exhaustion pulled him toward sleep. Shadows moved across the wall; he could count time only by his heavy, raucous breathing. Yet like the insidious scratching of a mouse in the ceiling, he heard other sounds. Female voices whispered. One said, "Has he fainted?" Another, "He's breathing." Mrs. Quill's voice said, clear as a bell, "Silas, I merely tried to wake you."

Out of his own breathing he awoke and it seemed that he might be dreaming. Two figures were in front of him, standing, not easily discernible in the gloom of the hallway.

Mrs. Quill and Jane looked down at him, though what he observed were only silhouettes. Slowly their faces appeared, abstract and difficult to interpret at first.

Mrs. Quill leaned over him, reaching forward to touch his shoulder, perhaps to help him to his feet, until their faces were almost level.

"Silas, you are ill . . ."

He stared at her face, attempting to read in her gray eyes and calm demeanor some explanation.

"I will be able to find my way back, madam." He paused to gather his strength. "You are leaving . . ."

Mrs. Quill nodded. "Yes."

"Not on my account, I hope."

"There is nothing for us here."

Mrs. Quill rose and half turned away. Something inside him rose with her.

"What are you fleeing from, madam?"

She did not answer for so long that he thought she would not.

"I have caused you damage. Now we must depart."

Mrs. Quill turned away finally toward the front door. She raised the latch and opened it. It let through a patch of light which fell on Grange's face. Jane passed through before her, a movement of shadows and light.

Grange stared at Mrs. Quill's remaining figure in the doorway. The open door let in light sufficient to hurt his eyes. Light gathered on her hair, her shoulders, and darkened her center.

He said, "I wish to thank you . . ."

Mrs. Quill had already turned away toward the door. Yet now she halted, frozen.

He experienced again that upward, eel-like movement of the soul, and began to rise to his feet with an effort. He stood, swaying. Mrs. Quill still did not move. As she looked out through the open doorway into daylight, her face became internal, blank.

Into the shadowy, empty space behind her Grange moved, halted facing toward her back, one hand against the wall to support himself. The light from the doorway on his face made him appear white. Even so, there seemed in his stance a sense of gathering strength. He spoke quite softly, as if he knew his words would bite into her soul.

"Why are you fleeing, madam? Is it because I woke you?"

Mrs. Quill closed her eyes for several seconds, then opened them. Standing behind her, he had no sense of the forces that moved within her. Her face became composed. It seemed to Grange that she passed through the door as softly as an angel. The latch clicked to with hardly a sound, and the light from the open door was extinguished on his face.

About the Author

WARWICK COLLINS' previous work includes the sailing thriller trilogy *Challenge*. He lives in Lymington, England.